# LOVE *in the* MOMENT
## *A memoir*

### *Text by*
# Karen Chien

### *Paintings by*
# Leland Lee

*Translated by Michele C. Chang*

*Edited & Designed by Steven Englander*

*Proofread by C. P. Chang*

Original edition published in paperback in Taiwan in 2014 by
Ping's Publications, Ltd., a division of Crown Culture Corporation.
This translated edition printed in Taiwan by Showwe Information Co., Ltd.
www.showwe.com.tw
publish@showwe.com.tw
ISBN 978-957-43-7537-0 (paperback)

*Title page: Dolphins.*
*Opposite page: Carnival, 2011, 16" x 21", marker on paper.*
*Front cover: Any Time Love, 2013, 50" x 38", acrylic on canvas.*

# Dedication

*To my childen,*
*Jason and Leland,*
*and my parents,*
*Mr. & Mrs. Archie Chien*

*Lord's Prayer, 2013, 36" x 29", acrylic on canvas.*

# Acknowledgments

My deepest appreciation for all the families with autism,
working so that all people can understand the spectrum
of this disability – including related disorders.
Like my own family, these devoted families
want all of us to focus on the ability.

*Snow Scene, 2009, 18" x 14", acrylic on canvas.*

# Contents

*Opposite page: Cinderella 1, 2006, 11" x 14", marker on cardboard.*

*A Butterfly Family in the Flowers*

# Introduction

## A perfect life—interrupted

Autism stormed into my world and interrupted my perfect life.

It is in my nature and upbringing to be an obedient daughter, a good student; a loving wife and a caring daughter-in-law. I always do what I'm supposed to do, I never thought I would be rebellious until I decided to move back to Taiwan from Los Angeles with Leland, against all odds. That decision was the first time I was defiant. I wanted to be myself – and a big part of me was already devoted to Leland.

When a child, I went to Dominican International School, Fuhsing Elementary School and Sacred Heart High School for Girls in Taiwan, then at age eighteen I went to the U.S. to study English Literature at the Univesity of California, Berkeley. Afterwards, I received my MBA degree from the Univesity of California, Los Angeles, majoring in Business. I also got a real estate license.

My life was very much by the book: study, work, marriage. Two years after college graduation, at age twenty-four, I married Philip Lee, an engineer working at the rocket center of Rockwell International. Philip Lee has a Master's degree from Stanford University.

After getting married, we had two children, Jason and Leland. My life had been on a smooth path, like a written script where I was destined to play a traditional woman's role. I did my best to fit the role to take care of everything so everyone in my life was pleased. This is how it appeared from an outsider's perspective.

Autism sneaked into my life like a thief, it stole the "perfect life" that I had meticulously established. Autism made me experience life's unpredictability and see life's imperfection. I was forced to enter into a labyrinth – with no way out.

When Leland was diagnosed with severe autism, I didn't know he was gifted in art; it never occurred to me that he would be in the one percent "autistic genius" category. Yet, my fighting spirit as a mother was ignited by the cruel fate that was dealt to me. I'm completely devoted to him; I make immeasurable efforts to defend him and help him to get rid of the "severe" label in hopes of moving forward to "normalcy," little by little.

**Part 1**
*My son has autism?*

*Previous pages: Any Time Gallop, 2014, 36" x 29", acrylic on canvas.*

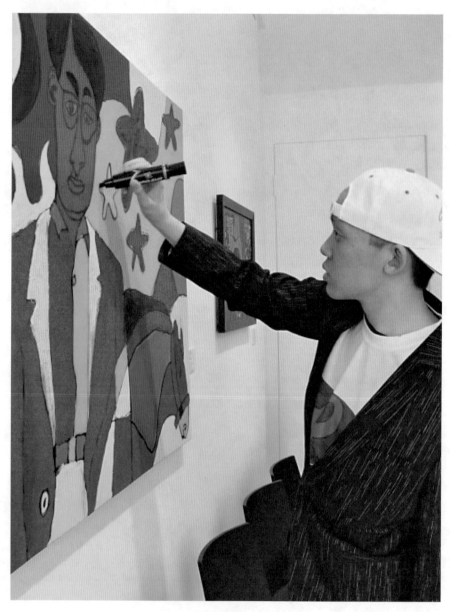

*Leland paints with concentration.*

# Sun and sunflowers

With a pen in hand, children usually like to scribble on any surface. Lines, circles, houses, the sky, or people with disproportional heads pop up freely. When they get tired, they throw away their pens and play with toys, or run outside to play with other kids. Every child in my community was the same. I enjoyed watching kids draw.

When Leland was a little older than one, his fingers had the jitters. But he was different. It seemed like overnight that he became a child who couldn't stop drawing, unless you pressed the stop button.

To press his stop button, every day I would carry Leland in my arms and take Jason, his 3-year-old brother, to join community play groups or sing-along programs. But whenever I didn't divert Leland's attention, his fingers would start to move in the air as if he was sketching, drawing the outline of imaginary objects.

What is the matter with this child? Didn't his mother teach him manners? The judgmental looks from people felt like needles pricking me. I thought to myself, "He can't keep doing this." I decided to buy drawing papers and coloring pens for him. Once he got those tools, he drew suns and sun-flowers with smiley faces in a matter of seconds. Later I realized that for him, the sky and sunflowers in our yard were probably the strongest visual objects he saw.

But having paper was not enough, he drew on walls, using vivid colors in a simplistic but bold way. I interpreted that activity as the pureness and brightness that comes from a child. Sometimes, when Jason, who shared the same room with him, had already fallen asleep, Leland was still awake and drawing on the wall. He stayed quiet, made no fuss and did nothing but draw, as if there was an angel whispering to him, "Draw! Draw! Just keep drawing!"

I think of the fairy tale from Hans Christian Andersen about a girl who, once she puts on her red dancing shoes, can't stop dancing. An angel says to the girl, "You have to dance! Wear your red dancing shoes and just dance!" The girl dances in the rain, under the sun and at night.

Does Leland also have a pair of red dancing shoes? Maybe coloring pens are his dancing shoes. But unlike The Red Shoes, which is a sad story, Leland's paintings are as bright as daylight.

*An angelic baby at six months.*

Jason probably found his little brother's behavior interesting, so he started to draw too. They used the walls in the bedroom as their canvas. In the beginning, I wiped their drawings away once they were done, but they would draw again the next day. After a while, I got tired of it and told myself, "Fine. Draw as you like. I'll see what the walls will be like."

One day, after a few years, I looked closely at the drawings. Even though there was nothing but sun and sunflowers, I could tell subtle differences between these new drawings and earlier ones. The new images looked like an animation with a simplistic story. I noticed Leland was not repeating the same drawing, he was expressing his thoughts in a methodical way.

Apart from drawing nonstop, he didn't speak and he didn't look at people. He had to smell everything and cried out loud when I bathed him with a shower head.

I told myself, "No problem. I can handle this; I will teach him and correct him. Everything will become normal as he grows up."

I didn't know that all those behaviors were signs of autism.

## My son has autism?

Before he turned one-and-a-half, my Leland was as adorable as an angel. When he was eighteen months old, he was diagnosed with autism.

It was my sister-in-law, Chun-Yan, who first noticed and alerted me when he was six months old. "Leland is a bit strange. He is different than other children," said Chun-Yan. Since she has three children, her experience and instinct enabled her to quickly sense if a child is unusual.

"How so?" I denied immediately. I didn't think that Leland was any different; I thought he was a perfect baby. I believed every baby has his/her unique personality, yet I didn't realize the uniqueness was signs of autism.

Jason was eighteen months older than Leland. Jason had behaved well and was an easy baby. Watching Jason growing up was the happiest time in my life, so I decided to have another child shortly.

*Leland and Karen on a horse farm.*

*Sun and Flowers. Are they Leland's first friends?*

As soon as Leland was one year old, he made the sound of "Nai Nai" (milk in Mandarin) when he wanted milk. He learned to express himself faster than Jason and exhibited a higher level of concentration. In the U.S., new clothes are sold with a price tag attached to the fabric. Leland would play with a price tag for hours, spinning it at different speeds and directions as if he was performing an experiment. I thought, "Wow! He will certainly become a scientist like his father in the future."

Before long, the entire family returned to Taiwan to celebrate my father-in-law's birthday. Chun-Yan reminded me again, "You must take Leland to see a doctor when you go back to the U.S."

After turning one and a half, Leland became a different baby. The original angel disappeared. Apart from gesticulating nonstop, he became very difficult, unreasonable and extremely attached to me. He would cry if he couldn't see me immediately. In addition, he vomited and had diarrhea frequently. I figured his crying was due to the sickness. Not sleeping well dwindled his spirit. He seemed like an old man living in a baby's body.

The problem of vomiting was severe. I had to change his clothes four or five times a day. When I couldn't dodge in time, he would throw up on my hair. In preparation for air travel, I prepared many sets of spare clothes but Leland threw up so much that we ran out of clean clothes to change into. When we went through an Immigration checkpoint with stinky clothes, the officers pinched their noses and talked with a heavy nasal sound, "Pass! Pass! Pass!" We didn't even have to have our luggage inspected!

Eventually, I came to the realization that something was indeed "wrong" with Leland; he was different from Jason. After returning to the U.S., I took Leland to UCLA Medical Center for a variety of neurodevelopmental evaluations at the Pediatric Psychiatry & Neurology departments. In the end, the diagnosis was that Leland has autism. The funny thing was, I had never heard of autism. "So. . . when will he recover? How does the treatment work?" I asked the doctor. The doctor said, "I'm afraid that Leland will not be able to talk or take care of himself." This was a response I didn't expect and thought I might have misheard. That serious? The prognosis was completely beyond my comprehension.

The word doctors used is "autism." In Taiwan, we translate the word into "self-enclosed disorder," and in China, people call it "loneliness disorder." The literal translation means one seals oneself off.

Why does my son have autism? What is the meaning of "one seals oneself off"? How is Leland going to grow up and live a normal life if he can't talk and take care of himself? I felt a bomb exploded and left me with nothing, while my heart ached so much it was as if someone had taken my heart, mangled it and trampled it on the ground.

*Leland at home, age six, drawing his favorite cowboys.*

When I left the hospital with Leland, I was so weak! I looked up into the sky, which was sunny, but I felt frigidly cold, like someone was lost in a snow blizzard.

That was in 1991, when I knew nothing about autism; no one had autism around me and no one talked about autism in general. I had never heard of Temple Grandin, let alone read her biography, "Emergence: Labeled Autistic," published in 1986. I hadn't seen the movie Rain Man. Autism was like a battle on the other side of the world, not relevant in my world. It wasn't until 1995, when Temple Grandin published "Thinking Pictures: My Life with Autism," that I learned how autistic patients think.

This is a long, unpredictable journey; even with light of increasing public awareness, we still have to fight the dark unknowns that are peeking around the corner. Life challenges will never cease; nevertheless, we have to go forward. As I am writing, a multitude of emotions well up, and comments about autistic children flood into my mind:

"They are a burden to the society!"

"He is autistic." Many people introduce Leland as such.

"He is a human being. He is not autistic."

Then Jason, Leland's older brother, would harshly and immediately correct them, as if Jason had turned into a Tyrannosaurus-Rex and his fury is about to lash out. I understand where Jason's rage comes from.

*After seeing an exhibit of Van Gogh's paintings at the Los Aangeles County Museum of Art, Leland painted Starry Starry Night.*

*Jason and Leland, going to a wedding in their Sunday best.*

Most people use their language indiscreetly. They are not aware that language reflects how they think. When people say "He is autistic," it has the connotation that his whole being is autistic and he is nothing but autistic. "He is autistic" is a very negative statement, implying shame and hopelessness. There is no cure, so no matter what we do will be in vain anyway.

However, saying "He has autism" has a completely different meaning. "He is a person with autism" suggests that they see not only autism but also his restrained abilities with certain expectations or understandings.

Every person who suffers from autism has different potential. To unleash the potential and develop their innate talents, start with small steps. Give them opportunities to learn and their potential can blossom; they will make tremendous progress. They can be first-rate quality controllers, bakers, computer engineers, landscape architects, pianists, artists or writers if they are provided with the correct kind of learning opportunities; if family members of autistic patients are persistent; if people develop an understanding of autism and accept it; and if society and government provide needed support systems.

The division of labor has become so convoluted in our society, everyone's life is interweaved with each other's and dependent on others to survive. People with autism are no exceptions.

# My father and life in Café Astoria

*Teen Karen with her parents.*

Before Leland was born and my life changed forever, people referred to me as the Café Astoria Princess whose life was carefree, who was pampered by her family.

My father, Archie Chien, was born in 1932 and was from the Xinzhuang district outside Taipei city.

My father always had a pioneering spirit. At the age of eight, shortly after his father passed away, he took a boat to Shanghai to visit his 30-year-old big brother and see the outside world. He stayed in Shanghai for over one month, taking in the bustling city with its trams and high-rise buildings; he then took a boat back to Taiwan with the impressions of the new world in his head.

In 1947, when my father was fifteen years old, the February 28 Massacre broke out in Taiwan, an anti-government uprising that was violently suppressed by the central government. By then my uncle had returned to Taiwan. He and my father took in more than 80 Chinese mainlanders. To provide them with food, my uncle asked my father to take his gold necklace to a pawn shop on Yanping North Road in exchange for supplies. My uncle said, "Helping others is helping yourself." This became the principle my father lived by, the principle I was taught as a little girl.

A smart Taiwanese boy, my father excelled at studying. He had followed his older brother's advice and studied English on his own. After graduating from Taipei's best boys high school, Jianguo High School, my father decided to forego university and stop being dependent on his big brother and sister-in-law. It is hard to say if that was a good or wrong decision, but once he made his choice, he never regretted it.

*Café Astoria, 2004, 14" x 11", marker on paper.*

Archie met several Russians who had taken refuge in Taiwan to escape World War II and communism. One of those Russians, Elsner, missed his hometown cooking dearly, especially the Russian-owned Astoria bakery on Xiafei Road in Shanghai.

My father was working on a housing construction project with the American Volunteer Group when Elsner convinced him to become partners and opened a western café and bakery, a turning point in my father's life.

*Karen with her father, Mr. Archie Chien.*

On October 30, 1949, Café Astoria opened at No. 7, Section 1, Wuchang Street, selling breads on the first floor and coffee on the second floor.

Eventually, he became the sole owner. Café Astoria created the first croissant and first chocolate cake in Taiwan as well as the legendary Russian soft candy. Whenever people ask about my beauty tips, I always reply that I was made with Russian soft candy and walnut cake in my mother's womb.

Featuring fine products and an exotic atmosphere, Café Astoria became the go-to place for celebrities. The mother of Shin Kong Group's founder, Ho-Su Wu, celebrated her 80th birthday at the café with the first layered cake ever made in Taiwan.

The highlight of every year was to make the birthday cake for President Chiang Kai-Shek. Back in the time when there were no luxurious hotels, when bakeries offered only two flavors, either cream or red beans, Café Astoria was chic. Its pastries were sumptuous products consumed by high society people.

Café Astoria is timeless due to its legacy; it carries the weight of continuing a piece of Taiwan's legacy for 70 years and for years to come. The third floor (where Leland holds his annual pizza party) was the location for countless social balls. I remember that I could join a formal ball only if I put on stockings and a pair of Sheng Sheng leather shoes, which was the top shoe brand at that time.

The Russian influence of Café Astoria connected my father to Nikolai, who used to study in Russia, and his wife, Faina. Their Chinese names are Chiang Ching-Kuo and Chiang Fang-Liang. Chiang Ching-Kuo was the son of President Chiang Kai-Shek and was President between 1978-1988.

I attended elementary school with their granddaughter, Maria; we practically grew up together. She would invite me to stay at their house and grandpa Chiang would read us stories and teach us how to write Chinese calligraphy. Sometimes I asked her to stay at my place and we would have girl's talk under the blankets; we developed a strong bond of sisterhood. As far as I'm concerned, this so-called dignitary family was nothing but a regular family who led a simple life.

My English name, Karen, was given to me by Elsner, whom my father called Uncle. At that time, he didn't know that Café Astoria would become the place where writers gathered, a base camp that created Taiwan's modern literary legacy. This relationship with literature began when my father helped a stranger who passed out in front of the café.

In 1959, a famous poet named Meng-Tieh Chou had opened a book-stand under an overhang in front of Café Astoria. My father didn't realize that the prostrate man, who looked like a skeleton, was actually the well-known poet. Due to a lack of business, the man hadn't eaten in three days and had fainted from hunger.

This encounter started a life-long friendship between my father and Meng-Tieh Chou. Out of admiration for Meng-Tieh Chou, an increasing number of his followers, such as writers and young artists, came to the café, drinking a cup of NT $6 coffee and staying all day to write. This led to Café Astoria to becoming the editors' base camp for the Literature Quarterly Publication. Consequently, my father was interrogated by the National Police about his association with the so-called left-wing writers who gathered in the café to work there.

Apart from "Helping others is helping yourself," I also learned about being "trustworthy" from my father. To him, once you make a promise – no matter whether or not there is a contract – you must do your best to deliver. If you can't, then don't guarantee lightly. My father hated those who don't keep their word.

I will always remember that we lived in the Qi Tiao Tong area when I was a child. Once, during a hurricane, the water rose up to my ankles on a street that was empty where it usually has heavy traffic. I watched my parents put on raincoats and walk into the rain; there were no taxis available, so they had to take a rickshaw. I looked at them from behind with anger. "Why must you work this hard? What is so important that you have to go out in hurricane weather?"

My father caressed my head and said, "A promise is a promise, even in hurricane weather, no excuses." Later, I learned that my father had agreed to deliver breads to stricken areas. If my father had been born in ancient China, he must have been the famous fool who had promised to meet a friend by a bridge. He held onto the pillars of the bridge with rising water. Eventually, this fool was drowned but he left behind a legend about trustworthiness.

In his later years, my father suffered a lot from heart diseases and was sent to the lintensive Care Unit several times. I can't remember how many times I signed hospital forms. Two out of three of his main arteries were completely calcified, but a passage was opened skillfully by Dr. Juey-Jen Hwang in the third artery. When my father was in the ICU, he would let the medical staff take care of him, but once transferred to the general ward, he always refused to let people help him. He would get up slowly from the hospital bed and wheel the intravenous bottle himself to use the bathroom before going back to bed.

After each hospital stay, even during the mandatory recovery period, my father maintained his routine of opening Café Astoria every morning at 7 o'clock, going home for lunch and a rest, then returning in the evening to close the café at 9 o'clock.

Despite his health, he always kept speech engagements that he had previously accepted. He didn't give in to any illness; it was not in his book to live in sorrow and complaints. He lived in dignity and didn't want to burden the family with special care and attention. My father had a strong will and did not let matters deter him: If I am sick, I don't lay in bed; if it rains heavily, I still go out.

He always had a sincere smile, looking calm and elegant. Whenever I persuaded him to rest, he would say he didn't want to waste his time, he wanted to live to the fullest every day while he was alive. His resilient character is like the common reeds, standing tall against the forces of wind. However, one would never know that his body was falling apart. He managed to escape death many times before passing away in 2018.

Being the little princess of Café Astoria, not only does my father's blood flow in me, I also inherited his persistence, willpower, and the traits to never complain and to stand up against injustice.

I was impatient and dominating but had softened under my father's teachings. My father knew my personality well, so he often said, "It would be great if you were a boy!"

Even though I am not a boy, several years ago I was honored to receive an inscription from the poet Meng–Tieh Chou:

 *Simplicity can conquer intricacy.*

 *Quiescence can overcome restlessness.*

 *Kindness can win people's hearts.*

He wrote those three lines based on my Chinese name and his understanding of my personality. I remind myself that this is the motto to live by for the rest of my life and to never give up.

God sees these potentials in me and my stubbornness to persevere, so He gave me life's most challenging assignment: Leland.

# What I know about autism

In 1910, the word "autism" was coined after the Latin word "autismus" by Swiss psychiatrist Eugen Bleuler, he applied the word to describe the inward, self-absorbed aspects of schizophrenia.

It hasn't been a long time since autism was confirmed as a disorder. In 1943, Doctor Leo Kanner from the U.S. published a seminal paper on autism, while Dr. Asperger from Vienna published his research results a year later.

Kanner was concentrating on children with severe autism, while Asperger was mainly focusing on autistic children with stronger language ability. Even though their research targets were different, both of their patients shared many of the same features. Therefore, this illness is named autism, which refers to a disorder in which patients show an extreme aloneness and do not respond to any stimulus from the outside world. A kind of self-isolation, a desire for aloneness and sameness, creating obstacles in communication and social interactions.

In his paper, Kanner described autistic children with an "inability to relate themselves in the ordinary way to people and situations from the beginning of life. . . There is from the start an extreme autistic aloneness that, whenever possible, disregards, ignores, shuts out anything that comes to the child from the outside."

In 1943, Leo Kanner wrote in "Autistic Disturbances of Affective Contact": "Another trait of the patients, insistence on sameness, creates demands not only the sameness of the wording of a request but also the sameness of the sequence of events. Lastly, autistic children have a peculiar and singular focus, they can become addicted and fixated on certain things."

Asperger described those patients he had observed as having "No eye contact with others, only brief glances. They barely have expression on their faces, don't have much body movements either. Their speech may sound peculiar due to abnormalities of inflection and a repetitive pattern. These children act on impulses and completely ignore their surroundings."

Before the 1980s, if you had a child with autism, you had to bear the brunt of the blame. The medical world assumed it was your impassive character, the way you raised the child, the possibility of mistreating your child that resulted in your child's obstacle in learning and communicating.

*National Museum of History [Taipei], 2013, 16" x 20", acrylic on canvas.*

Some children even mutilate themselves, have no sense of feces and would smear them everywhere. The image of the "refrigerator mother" proved indelible in the public imagination. For a long time, autism was considered psychogenic, triggered by mothers who failed to love and nurture their children so the children retreated into a self-enclosed condition. Also for a long time, autism was seen as schizophrenia.

As for treatment, there were many bizarre techniques. There was even a method of squeezing a child in a quilt so the child could re-experience the process of birth from the birth canal. Some children died from suffocation in the process.

Ivar Lovaas, a psychology professor from UCLA who has been studying autistic children for over thirty years, defines autism as "social awkward-ness. . . Social awkwardness is the definition of autism, which is the common problem for all the children with autism. Despite variance in

*Dance, 2009. 24" x 18", marker on paper.*

intelligence and emotional engagement issues, they share the same in delayed social development."

Autism can't be generalized. From mental retardation to genius with an IQ of 160 or higher, from not being able to talk and not able to take care of oneself to mild Asperger Syndrome that people hardly notice, the autistic group includes people from both sides of the spectrum. Their developmental paths vary since conditions are unique to each person.

For children who are diagnosed with autism during infancy and get an early start in treatment, some of them can have obvious improvements in their language abilities and even have a 180-degree turn so they converse regularly, play with peers and have interactions. Still, there is a lack of social understandings and awkwardness in communication with others as well as difficulty distinguishing subjects and objects.

When things interest them, their way of learning shows a deeper level of focus and concentration; they can excel and outperform others. Conversely, they show difficulty in learning or not being able to focus on things of disinterest. This kind of child is classified as "high-functioning autism" or "Asperger Syndrome," which belong to the same spectrum as autism.

When society talks about autism, people usually put their focus on "high-functioning autism." There are many incredible stories about high-functioning autistic people.

The book "Shadow Syndromes" by John Ratey, M.D. and Catherine Johnson, Ph.D., is about a little girl with high-functioning autism. This girl has high intelligence and speaks fluently. Although she isn't diagnosed with autism until eight years old, she can read lengthy novels above her age group. However, when the girl joins a soccer team, after walking onto the field with other teammates, she doesn't move, doesn't run after the ball or run with others. When Mom asks her why she doesn't move, she replies that she thought she is supposed to kick the ball when the ball stops in front of her feet.

People with autism don't understand why others play in groups and have so much fun; why a group of people would gather and chat about everything and anything. They don't have the concept of sharing. Researchers observed that when they took away a toy from an autistic child, he didn't object. Along the same line, he didn't understand why he had to share the toy with another child or play together. If other children pull his hair or pinch his arm, an autistic child will not fight back unless he is taught repeatedly to fight back.

Dr. Temple Grandin has autism. She fought a lot when she was a kid. Today she is a professor of Animal Science at Colorado State University. She is an important person in my life who helped me tremendously.

There are people among us with less obvious autistic syndrome. They are usually labeled as a nerd, weirdo, geek, dork, etc. Many works in high tech domains. The Massachusetts Institute of Technology (MIT) started to offer a course so those students who are gifted in mathematics and science but clumsy at social events could learn social skills.

Some people with mild autism can have normal relationships, get married, have children, have a career; there are even some wives who learn that their husbands have autism only after being married for a long time.

Leland is not that fortunate. To date, he can only carry simple conversations, living in a world secluded from relationships and interaction with the ever-changing society.

Even today the medical profession hasn't yet found the root cause of autism. There is a hypothetical link to vaccinations: that children were born normal, then started to have symptoms after a year and a half old. However, most doctors, scientists and researchers believe that autism is a primary and random syndrome due to a congenital anomaly in the brain, related to certain genes, and has nothing to do with the child's upbringing.

Since the cause is unknown, the medical world defines autism based on external behaviors. According to textbooks, the three main characteristics are difficulty in communication and social skills, plus repetitive behaviors. More or less, most people on the spectrum have some traits of those three features.

Autism Spectrum Disorder (ASD) is a large spectrum of similar disorders of social, cognitive, language and motor development. In 2018, the U.S. Center for Disease Control determined that approximately 1 in 59 children is diagnosed with an autism spectrum disorder; the World Health Organization stated 1 in 160 children has an autism spectrum disorder.

The male-female ratio of typical autism is about four to one, while the male-female ratio of Asperger Syndrome is nine to one. There are forty-seven million people with ASD in the world.

In Taiwan, the Ministry of Health and Welfare shows that the ASD population is 14,000 people in 2018.

The puzzling and troubling fact is that the autistic population is still increasing.

*Monkey on the Swing, 2009.*

*This page, clockwise from upper left: Starry Night in Moscow, 2012, 15" x 18", acrylic on canvas; Miles Davis; Meditation, 2005, 16" x 20", acrylic on cnvas; Giraffes, 2009, 16" x 20", acrylic on canvas.*

# But how does it happen?

There are trillions of cells in a human body, chromosomes in cell nuclei and genes in chromosomes; genes are comprised of long or short sections of DNA. There are hundreds of billions of neurons in our brain. How do they work so we remember who we are, learn, think and dream? Why do we have feelings of passion or anger? How do we learn to ride a bicycle or understand the meaning of words? How do we distinguish our mother's voice in a crowd? Patients with schizophrenia, depression, Alzheimer's disease, multiple sclerosis, chronic pain syndrome, paralysis. . . what went wrong with their neural connections?

Dr. Douglas Fields, author of "The Other Brain," has opened the door to the neuroscience field of glial cell function. Fields is currently Chief of the Nervous System Development and Plasticity Section at the National Institutes of Health and is an international authority on brain development, neuron–glia interactions, and the cellular mechanisms of memory. However, he didn't include autism.

For the moment, the research that is closest to the truth is from a team at the University of North Carolina at Chapel Hill, which published in 2013 an article in Nature, an international academic weekly journal of science. The report suggests there is a type of enzyme called Topoisomerase in everyone's body. If the structure of Topoisomerase is damaged, it is possible to cause collateral damage to long genes that could cause autism and other illnesses associated with neural development. Hsien-Sung Huang, assistant professor at the Graduate Institute of Brain and Mind Sciences at National Taiwan University, also participated in this research.

Simply put, autism is a neuropathic abnormality hindering the nervous system from normal development. Neurons that receive, process and transmit information through electrical and chemical signals don't function as usual, as if they are out–of–bound balls. Patients' cognitive abilities are inhibited; their minds don't work the same, some are over–sensitive to touch and sound; some are obsessed with lines, light and shadow; some can't stop shaking, some have a photographic memory; some suffer from ADHD; the extreme cases can hurt themselves without feeling pain or can't differentiate between cleanliness and filth. Everyone's symptoms are different, but almost all have three obvious symptoms: difficulty in communication, repetitive actions and social obstacles.

All the symptoms of autism are developmental. The conditions vary from person to person with a wide range in the spectrum. Autism won't go away as the patients age. They won't start to talk, be able to understand people, have normal cognitions, or tell you their inner feelings overnight. The game changer lies in education, life experiences and training in social skills. Start by eliminating the fear of smells and sounds, then other fears, to allow them to move in stages of learning. Only those with severe autism need lifelong and special care.

Dr. Wen-Che Tsai from Children's Mental Health Center at National Taiwan University Hospital, pointed out an animal experiment in Italy. That research discovered a type of cell called "mirror neuron" in the brain of primate monkeys that enables monkeys to imitate each other. Human brains also have the same mirror neurons; therefore, babies can imitate and learn from their parents' actions. Autistic children lack the capability of understanding other's thinking, they don't know how to "read" people's emotions. It is possible that their mirror neurons are thinner than normal, affecting the transmission of information and resulting in poor perception with oversensitivity in touch, hearing and other senses.

The million-dollar question: "Is autism hereditary?"

There is no definitive answer. There is one statement suggesting that only 3% of autism is related to heredity and the other causes are unclear. However, Simon Baron-Cohen, Professor of Developmental Psychopathology at the University of Cambridge as well as Director of the Autism Research Center, published a study in 2012 called Autism and The Technical Mind. The conclusion is, "Children of scientists and engineers may inherit genes that not only confer intellectual talents but also predispose them to autism."

Baron-Cohen conducted a study involving nearly 2,000 families in the U.K. He included about half these families because they had at least one child with autism. The other families had children with a diagnosis of Tourette Syndrome, Down Syndrome or language delays – but not autism.

The study team asked parents in each family a simple question: What was their job? Many mothers had not worked outside the home, so they could not use the mothers' data, but the results from fathers were intriguing: 12.5 percent of fathers of children with autism were engineers, compared with only 5 percent of fathers of children without autism. Likewise, 21.2 percent of grandfathers of children with autism had been engineers, compared with only 2.5 percent of grandfathers of children without autism.

*Ball Game, 2007, 24" x 24", acylic on canvas.*

Coincidence? Is this data meaningful? Baron-Cohen doesn't think it's a coincidence. One possibility is that the genes responsible for autism persist, generation after generation, because they are co-inherited with genes underlying certain cognitive talents common to both people with autism and technical-minded people whom some might call geeks.

All systems follow rules. When you systemize, you identify the rules that govern the system so you can predict how that system works. This fundamental drive to systemize might explain why people with autism love repetition and resist unexpected changes.

Another possible explanation involves a phenomenon known as assortative mating, which usually means "like pairs with like." But when scientists and engineers pair up and have kids, their children may get a double dose of autism genes and traits. In this way, assortative mating between technical-minded people might spread autism genes. Some people claim that Silicon Valley in California has autism rates 10 times higher than the average for the general population.

Leland's father happens to be an engineer.

However, Dr. Susan Gau from National Taiwan University doesn't agree with this theory. She has researched more than seven hundred autistic families in Taiwan. However, the parents' occupations don't trend to technical-minded professions, but spread equally to all walks of life. In addition, the parents have different educational backgrounds as well as different social status.

The second million-dollar question: "Is there a cure for autism?"

The biological mechanism of autistic patients is more complicated than we imagine. The abnormality varies from person to person. More than half of high-functioning autistic grown-ups suffer from anxiety and panic disorders; problems with allergies are common, and dysfunction of intestinal movement, resulting in severe pain.

So far, clinicians can only use medications to manage individual symptoms, such as hyperactivity, depression, panic, anxiety, obsessive compulsive disorder, etc. Some medications can indeed relieve the extent of sensitivity, stop distracting thoughts, and improve behaviors and interpersonal interactions. But at the same time, biochemical medications usually come with serious side effects, such as insomnia, agitation or aggressive behaviors. I am more inclined to believe in faith and the healing power of nature.

*Seahawk, 2010, 12" x 16", acrylic on wood.*

In the beginning of 2013, Norovirus was epidemic in Taiwan. Leland and I both were infected. We had fever, diarrhea and vomiting. At the hospital, we were both having intravenous injections when Leland – out of nowhere – asked me, "Mommy, are we going to heaven today?" I tried to answer him with a smile, "One day, but not today." Then I immediately turned my head to the other side; I didn't want him to see my tears welling up.

Why me? How did this happen? There is no answer. I know we will go to heaven one day, but not today. I am determined to be a woman of faith, relying on God's grace to give me strength to walk with Leland longer and further on this journey.

# Every "Rain Man" is unique

In my eyes, people on the spectrum of ASD are the special breed among us. Unique, original, completely genuine, they are different than others. The more I see them, the more I feel this way.

— Dr. Oliver Sacks

"Hey! Why are you shutting yourself out?"

"I never want to leave the house, am I autistic?"

"My cat must have autism. It hides itself whenever visitors come."

"I got the autism!"

Every time I hear people indiscreetly or half-jokingly using the word "autism," my heart trembles with pain, as if one can choose autism or not, or it is contagious. But acts of deliberate, self-inflicted, or acquired behaviors are not in the medical definitions of autism. Given the hostile meaning of autism, parents of autistic children in Taiwan advocate the term Kanner's Syndrome instead of autism.

In 2011, Leland, his father and I were interviewed by the Good TV channel in Taipei. The title they gave Leland was "Rain Man the Genius."

I find that most people's perception of autism is from the movie Rain Man, which was directed by Barry Levinson and starred Dustin Hoffman and Tom Cruise. Released in 1988, Dustin Hoffman won the Academy Award's Oscar™ for Best Actor in a Leading Role. Until now, Rain Man has been synonymous with autism.

Dustin Hoffman's character, Rain Man (he mispronounces his name Raymond as "Rain Man"), has the ability to memorize everything, including phone directories, television programs and all sorts of information. But he doesn't understand what the information is about or know what to do with it. He moves around stiffly while his behaviors are awkward. He lives with a strict daily schedule, eats the same food on the same day of the week and buys the same underwear. If anything disrupts his routine, he is likely to panic, scream or knock his head against the wall, or hit his head. The sound of an alarm bell is one noise he cannot bear.

Rain Man is a true story inspired by a person named Kim Peek, but the movie does not reflect his life story. Kim Peek was born in 1951 in Salt Lake City, Utah, with damage to the cerebellum, a condition in which the bundle of nerves that connects the two hemispheres of the brain is missing. He was diagnosed by his doctor with severe mental retardation: he would never learn to walk, talk or take care of himself, so his mother and father were told to institutionalize their son in a nursing home.

But Peek's parents didn't follow the doctor's suggestion. Kim was able to memorize things from the age of 16-20 months. Every time he finished a book, he could retain up to 98% of the content. What's more surprising is that Kim read by scanning the left page with his left eye, then the right page with his right eye. On average, he could read two pages every 8-10 seconds, as if he was a scanning machine which would never crash, and his memory bank carried twelve thousand books. He also had a calendar-calculating skill whereby he could quickly tell you, for any given date whatsoever, which day of the week it fell upon.

However, apart from those capabilities, everything about Kim conformed to the doctor's prediction. Kim couldn't button up his shirts, he was un-steady when he walked, and he only scored 87 on the intelligence test (the score for average people is 100 and a score above 130 is rated as a genius). But Kim's memory IQ was 220.

Because of Rain Man, Kim became a public figure and was invited to give speeches in the U.S. as well as in other countries. With the increase in pub-lic exposure, his social skills improved and Kim developed new confidence in meeting people and addressing audiences.

In 2009, Kim Peek died of a heart attack at the age of fifty-eight. His history proves that autistic patients can make up for congenital defects with teachings and trainings.

In 2006, Daniel Tammet, an autistic savant, wrote a book, "Born on a Blue Day," which attracted attention in the U.S. At the beginning of the book, he mentions Rain Man:

> "I'm much like Raymond which is portrayed by Dustin Hoff-man. I have a compulsive need for order and routine and that affect almost every aspect of my life. For instance, I eat precisely 45 grams of cereal for breakfast every morning and I would use an electronic scale to make sure that it is the exact amount.

"Then, I cannot leave the house without counting the number of items of clothing I'm wearing. I would get very anxious if I don't drink tea at the same time every day. When I get stressed or am unhappy, I close my eyes and counts. Thinking about numbers can calm me down."

Tammet can recite π (Pi) from memory to 22,514th digits. He is also a genius in languages and learned conversational Icelandic in a week.

The popularity of Rain Man makes Raymond (or mostly Dustin Hoffman) the representative of autism that the public perceives: weird, retarded, not all together; can't perform simplest things to meet one's needs – but at the same time has super-natural capabilities. The problem is that Rain Man has autism but does not represent autism.

*Every autistic patient is unique.* The condition "presents" differently in different patients. How these patients think and process information varies as well. In medicine, Raymond is classified as an "autistic genius" or "idiot genius." All the Raymond's in the world represent only one percent among autistic patients; seventy percent of autistic patients have mental retardation and don't have any jaw-dropping ability to be made into movies or be written about in books. That is the real autism. The portrayal of "autistic prodigies" misleads the public about autism as well as the needs of 90 percent of autistic patients.

Compared to autistic people possessing special abilities, such as Kim Peek, people with mild autism but no unusual skills are not easily recognized. Even so, they are usually labelled as "hard to get along," "not all together," or "no EQ (Emotional Quotient)" in group settings.

Occasionally an autistic character is in a movie or TV series. But this doesn't help the public to have a better understanding of autism. The most depressing situation is for a "normal" actor to imitate autistic behaviors to amuse people. Documentaries of autistics are closer to reality than fictional portrayals.

The documentary Twinkle Twinkle Little Stars, directed by Zheng-Cheng Lin, is about four autistic children and their families in Taiwan. The kids, including Leland, all have a gift for painting and are mostly high-functioning autistic patients. After more than one year of filming and interacting with the patients, Zheng-Cheng Lin shared his thinking:

"What's the relationship between these special children and the social system established by the so-called normal people? We teach them our patterns of behavior and social lifestyles, all in the name of "for their own good" so they can conform to the standards defined by the majority.

"However, is it possible that their natural language, behavior, thinking and ways of expressing emotions are misled? Or the ways for them to communicate with the rest of the world are misdirected, diminishing the value of their existence. . . Autistic patients are unable to blossom, to live a life the natural way."

Children from the Distant Planet, directed by Ke-Shang Chen, penetrates into the isolated inner world of autistics, providing the audience an insight into the difficulty autistics have with external communication and often being misunderstood. A Rolling Stone, another documentary directed by Ke-Shang Chen, won first prize at the Taipei Film Festival in 2013, continues to confront issues about autism.

In A Rolling Stone, the lens focused on a caregiver, the father of an autistic man, presents the dark side of autistic patients. The 30-year-old Li-Fu Chen has a hoarding addiction, in which he collects every kind of waste paper, as well as bricks and bee honeycombs. He is immersed in his own world, he talks to himself, he pounds the table when he is angry, he swears at his father and sometimes uses violence on him.

*Virginia Tree, 2013, 16" x 16", acrylic on canvas.*

*San Francisco, 2013, 16" x 20", marker on wood.*

The 60-year-old father, Hong-Dong Chen, was determined to fulfill his responsibility by providing for the family. But he often is emotionally drained and physically exhausted. "I'm not a person with greatness." "We are just ordinary people." "Can I give up?" he says to the camera. Therefore, when the director was interviewed, he said that he simply couldn't give the film a touching ending with heartwarming music.

In my opinion, autistic families are facing new challenges every day, fighting every day. We need more empathy, more understanding, more resources to provide to adults with autism so they can live out their lives. I hope every parent with autistic children – including myself – can wake up with a smile every day.

I once read in the Taiwan United Daily News how a 22-year-old student sued his teacher due to the comments on his report card: "stubborn, closed-minded, anti-social, no people skills." Did that teacher ever think that the problem might be caused by bad neuron connections behind the scenes? In other words, EQ is a natural gift that you have feelings, have the ability to feel what others feel, also the ability to express yourself properly. It is the same as whether you have talent in sports or not. You're born with it. You can improve with training and practices but you can't train a person who has no talent in sports into an Olympic athlete.

In Washington D.C. I met an autistic savant who works as a political journalist at a newspaper office. He is an expert in history and politics and relies on others to help him with daily chores; otherwise, everything would be a mess. In any conversation, no matter if you're interested or not, regardless of what you ask, he just talks about history and politics. A conversation with him is like a squash game, except we each play with our own ball in the same court.

The only two subjects ever on his mind are history and politics. But if you don't know the reason for his behavior, you would be irritated by his rudeness and want to give him a piece of your mind or a whack on his head!

In some ways humans are not free; we are bound by the complex compositions of our body. But the reason we are human beings is because we are able to advance, revamp, have breakthroughs, learn to avoid "amygdala hijack" conditions where one can't think clearly, make rational decisions, or control our own responses. Unfortunately, Leland has severe autism and those abilities are a long reach for him.

**Part 2**
*I wish the drawing
would stop*

*Amsterdam, 2013, 36" x 29", acrylic on canvas.*

# Learn to brush teeth with Polaroid

Every time I look back on how I stumbled along the way in raising a child with autism, my heart aches. So many tears I shed at night, the constant fear I had, the hurt I felt with every slur after Leland became famous. "Your accomplishment is only possible in a rich family" is like adding salt to a wound.

After confirming that Leland had severe autism, the only word that can describe my mental state would be "insanity." I was ignorant and arrogant. I told myself, "Autism is like the flu, maybe a severe flu. As long as I find the best doctor, get the best treatment, my child can most certainly be cured within months or maybe a few years." The power of maternal love is invincible and can move heaven and earth. A mother would do anything for her child, she becomes a fearless fighter.

The first step I took was taking Leland to the Department of Health, hospitals and schools to collect information regarding autism. I needed to understand what autism is and find known treatments. There were very few books written for parents of autistic children at that time. Despite my great efforts, I had limited success so I had to turn to doctors. Doctors redirected me to the libraries and information on microfilm. I had to enlarge the microfilms in order to print the articles. I was overjoyed, as if I hit the jackpot. I read every word carefully. The internet didn't exist thirty years ago, so I had to read research papers on individual case studies like a hard-working student.

A distracting murmur would cross my mind every now and then. "You should focus on your career. There is no cure for autism anyway, so don't waste your time." But I've never swerved.

The U.S. is known for its strength in medicine, but old wive's tales and alternative treatments are still being practiced. I did them all. I tried Chinese medicine, western medicine, mainstream treatments and alternative ways. Someone suggested acupuncture, so Leland did it; another person said that traditional Chinese medicine worked, so Leland was treated that way; I even heard that yoga and gymnastics could do wonders. To sum up, from the U.S. to Europe, I kept my ears open: as long as it was within my means, I would give any treatment a try.

The terminology for teaching autistic children is called Discrete Trial Training (DTT). For example, if you want to teach a boy the word "door," you take him to a real door, point at the door and say "door." But it doesn't require doing this only once or twice, you must teach him repeatedly. However, the child has no ability to draw inferences; when he sees different kinds of doors, those procedures need to be repeated.

Teaching autistic children is like doing drills, step-by-step with repetitions. "Door," "water," "dog," "school" – I racked my brain to find ways to teach him vocabulary. Until Leland was three years old, he could only make some sounds and say certain words, he couldn't speak a complete sentence.

Every time he wanted something, he grabbed my finger to point at it. For example, in order to teach him the word "tang" ("candy" in Mandarin), I had to be resolute and not give him candy directly. Whenever I pushed him to pronounce "tang," he would sound out words like "mang" (busy), "da" (hit), which sounds similar to "tang." "Tang, tang, tang," I repeated once, twice, three times or even more till he could pronounce it correctly.

From a single word to a complete sentence is even more difficult. For example, from "cup" and "water" to "use the cup to drink water." Smartphones didn't exist twenty years ago, but I bought a Polaroid camera to capture a variety of cups and tell him that they are all cups. Then, I grabbed his hand to pat on the water to connect cups with water so he could understand that the cups are used for drinking water.

Next step: I taught him daily routines after waking up in the morning. "Go to the toilet," "brush teeth," "wash face," "change clothes." I photographed each step with the Polaroid and pasted the photos in the order matching the task on a board: get off the bed, walk to the bathroom, pee in the toilet, walk to the mirror, use toothbrush and toothpaste to brush teeth, rinse the mouth. I used seven photos to teach him how to brush his teeth and it took him eight months to learn it.

We had a routine for leaving the house. First, put on the shoes, so I had photos of shoes; then, the car ride, so I had photos of my car as well. Once Leland learned the routine, when I said, "We are going out," he knew to put on shoes and go to the car. That's right, every detail in daily life needed to be taught. Many trivial things are a snap for normal children—but incredibly hard for Leland. Put it this way: 100 meters to others would become 1,000 or even 10,000 meters for Leland. If I didn't teach him as much as possible before five years old, which is the time that the cranial nerves develop rapidly, 1,000 or 10,000 meters would become 100,000 meters – or even unreachable.

*Blue Jay in the Woods, 2004, 31" x 30", acrylic on canvas.*

## Race against time

I had to race against time. These words rang in my head at all times:
"I must maximize Leland's prime-learning years." I was worried that if I
slacked off, Leland would lag behind.

There were reasons that Leland couldn't learn: sometimes because of
fear. Leland is afraid of babies; maybe it's because of their crying, or they
look like "aliens" in his eyes. After noticing that he was afraid of babies,
I took a lot of pictures to show him until he was used to seeing babies.
Whenever we encounter a real baby, I would take his hand to touch the
baby saying, "Baby smells so nice!" "Baby is so soft!" When the baby cried,
he would withdraw his hands right away and take two steps back. I had to
tell him immediately that the baby cries because baby is hungry or diaper is
wet. Little by little, with repetitions to help him believe babies smell good,

*Kind Moose Singing*

babies are soft and they are not horrible. Thirty years passed by – and he is still afraid of crying babies!

Despite my tireless efforts, Leland didn't talk. Since he didn't talk, I talked. Every night before bedtime, I read stories to him, whether he understood or not, whether he wanted to listen or not. We would check out books and tapes from the library. I would repeat a story ten times, a hundred times. I told him that if he builds a house on sand, it would be destroyed by wind; I said that Snow White ate a poisonous apple.

He always listened quietly, unlike other kids with nonstop questions: "What happens next?" "And then?" "Why?" I never knew if he liked the Three Little Pigs or Snow White. A long time passed. One day out of the blue, Leland recited the stories I had told him. I realized he had actually listened to every single word of the stories and stored them all in his memory.

When Leland was three and a half years old, he could go to kindergarten according to local regulations. Running between schools every day, I was like a madwoman. One was a special education school subsidized by the government; another was a normal school. I hired a private tutor to teach Leland how to talk.

I followed a doctor's suggestion to use only English to communicate, thinking multiple languages would be too confusing for Leland. But this method turned out to be a huge mistake for older brother Jason, who lost the chance to learn Chinese. Jason was even confused about his identity, thinking he was Jewish at one point!

This error will continue to be a regret throughout my life. However, when Leland moved to Taiwan with me in 2006, he learned Mandarin and Taiwanese, proving he could learn more than one language. In retrospect, I realized another mistake: I was too arrogant, too ambitious. I thought I was strong enough to shoulder everything, but whenever I used all my energy yet saw that Leland was still marching in the same spot, I became frustrated, weak, lonely and lost. Those emotions surrounded me like multiple layers of heavy fog.

When I had doubts about my ability in caring for Leland, God found me and came into our lives. He gently put us into the palm of His hands. It seemed He was telling me, "Everything will be OK. Leland is also my child, whom I cherish. We will love him together."

# Charging ahead but going nowhere

People say that the biggest achievement for a mother is to see her children leave the nest. Jason left the nest, yet Leland is a bird that can never fly. When he went to school, I was in school with him. The first school he attended, along with Jason, was the kindergarten of UCLA. Among his classmates were the goddaughter of Barbara Streisand, the daughter of Arnold Schwarzenegger, the son of Steven Spielberg, et al. It was a celebrity's kindergarten that adopted an open and play-based learning approach. There was even a small farm inside the kindergarten.

Normally UCLA does not accept students like Leland. But timing was on my side: there was a research project to integrate autistic children into a normal school. Plus, I am an alumna. Leland became their first autistic student, a guinea pig in the research. How did this guinea pig perform?

For kids around that age, usual activities were lining up, holding hands, dancing, playing games or quiet activities like cutting, pasting, reading stories, watching cartoons. But Leland couldn't understand the teachers' instructions. He would stand while others were sitting, he would paint while others were dancing. He often cried and screamed unexpectedly out of frustration.

From the start, I had to sit next to him and be his personal interpreter. My presence would calm him down. Nonetheless, the teachers excluded him and didn't pay much attention to him. When I complained to the teachers in a nice way, they argued, "He needs to learn to be independent!" Life is full of unexpected twists and turns: twenty years later, the Director of that project turned out to be Jason's graduate school advisor.

If it wasn't for Leland, Jason wouldn't have gone on the path of studying autism. He earned a Master's degree from UCLA in autism research, was a youth pastor and became a seminary student in 2019. I think he would have become a violinist, a computer programmer, or a marine biologist – all of which he loved. The day when Jason told me he was going to study psychology in order to help autistic children, I couldn't help thinking: Did Leland and I rob Jason's freedom? He couldn't be free to do whatever his heart desired? More than once I told Jason, "You are so brilliant and gifted in many ways. You have your own life so you shouldn't give up what you truly love for your little brother. You don't have to carry your little brother." Frankly, if I could have stopped him, I wouldn't have allowed him to study autism. I didn't want the whole family consumed by autism. I have even thought about whom I can entrust Leland to when he doesn't have a family to rely on.

Yet Jason rebelled against me in the end and walked into the world of autism. After entering graduate school, he frequently drove two hours just to teach an autistic child. Once, he had an aggressive encounter in which he was bitten. I asked him, "Why do you want to do this? Don't you think Leland and I suffer enough already?" His answer was so brief and firm that I couldn't dispute it. "Because this is a very meaningful thing." However, not every teacher views teaching as "meaningful" nor has the capacity to love and teach students like their own children.

Some teachers are like angels, whereas others don't have passion. They regard teaching as just a job; they don't know how to care for children with special needs. In kindergarten, Leland was a special case under observation. Every teacher knew that but they didn't have the patience to pay extra attention to him; of course, they also lacked the experience in teaching autistic children. Several teachers chose to ignore him, others intentionally didn't look at him, and a few didn't call his name—they simply ignored his existence.

Children in the classroom were quick to observe their teachers' behavior and could tell that the teachers didn't like this kid; therefore, classmates stayed away from Leland. No one took the initiative to play with him. Every day, I watched Leland playing with sand and water, drawing quietly by himself. As long as I was there, he wouldn't cry and scream.

A kid who was treated as if he was invisible like air, an unwanted person. Were his feelings hurt? Did this experience leave a scar in his heart? Was this exclusion an act of discrimination or silent bullying?

I also became the person that the teachers disliked. They considered me as a "watchdog." Therefore, I had to try my best to refrain from intervening. I tried to let go little by little, from holding him in my arms in class to sitting in the rear of the class. Then I let him stay in the class alone, telling him that Mommy had to assist in other classes. But I had to bring him to the next class, to let him know that Mommy is close by. During each break, I ran to his class to check if there was someone bullying him, and also to

*Hand Prints, 2010, 30" x 90", acrylic on canvas.*

let him know that Mommy was there all the time. Not seeing me or not knowing where I am, Leland would look for me anxiously. To this day, he still behaves like this.

After "experimenting" for eight months, I can't say it was a complete waste of time. Leland learned to sit in the classroom quietly, although he didn't absorb everything. He could also go to the canteen to eat lunch with his classmates and put away his fork and knife after a meal, which is the required discipline in a group life.

However, apart from this few developments, the entire experience proved that Leland couldn't learn in that kind of environment, let alone make progress. He needed teaching that could coordinate with his way of learning. Otherwise, it would be like what the Red Queen from Alice in Wonderland said, "Run as fast as we can, just to stay in place."

I decided to try other methods. The mother of the Chinese philosopher, Mencius, moved her family three times in search of a better learning environment for her son. Mencius was often described as the "Second Sage," after Confucius. Thankfully, there are automobiles in the 20th century. To find a good teacher for Leland, I drove back and forth on the highways, trying one school after another. My search efforts paid off when we found Barbara, an excellent teacher.

# Barbara, beloved teacher

When Leland was three years old, after asking around, I learned that Barbara Killian was well known for teaching autistic children in West Los Angeles. She taught a special class designed for autistic children between 3-10 years old at Westwood Charter School.

The first time I visited Barbara with Leland, she told me she already had eight children in her class, so she couldn't take more and asked me to go home. But I didn't give up easily. I pressed on and asked her help to come up with solutions. In the end, she had to tell me, "Leland's mother, I'll tell you what, I want to retire." Using retirement to get rid of me? She didn't expect that I would not go away.

One week later, I visited her again with Leland. I begged her in the same way and she still didn't agree. In order to make progress, I made a concession. "Then could you please give me suggestions on which school I should take Leland to?" This time, she looked at me and said, "You come over after a few weeks."

Her words gave me hope. After a couple of weeks, I returned with Leland. "But you are not in this school district," she said. "You need to register first and enter into the lottery," she ordered in a business-like manner.

I followed her instructions and waited for the lottery. But every Thursday at noon, I would wait outside Barbara's classroom on the dot. I knew it was her lunchtime. After the break, as soon as she came out of the classroom, she would see us.

When she was not smiling, Barbara looked stern. Every week, I went to see this unfriendly face. One day when the weather was scorching hot, I waited for her for so long that I kept sweating. She scolded me, directly into my face. "You are still here? Are you crazy?"

"Please help my son," I replied.

That was a magical day. After two years, my persistence paid off, like a hardened ice starting to melt; a locked door which couldn't be opened became wide open. All of a sudden, I was in! Barbara and I became good friends and our friendship lasts till today. Whenever we go to our house in Los Angeles, Leland and I would visit her, our dear Barbara. It was Barbara who discovered Leland's unique talent.

*Barbara Killian and Leland*

# Saturn

The two years between UCLA kindergarten and Barbara's class were a turbulent period. Leland and I were drifting from one school to another; we tried six schools. We also went to a church school close to home. The teachers were indifferent, so we only stayed there for one semester. Some schools had good teachers but the classmates had behavioral problems. I was worried that Leland would imitate his classmates, using swear words or hitting people, so we didn't stay long. I heard there was a reputable male special education teacher in downtown Los Angeles, so I wanted to send Leland there. But Leland's father Philip was against this idea; some relatives and friends also said I was crazy. My premise was that choosing teachers is more important than picking schools or deciding on school districts. I insisted on transferring Leland to this teacher's class.

That school is called Saturn Elementary School. Every kid has a lesson to learn about the planet Saturn when they attend this school. Leland therefore has a connection with Saturn and that is the reason why he has a series of paintings of Saturn.

The school was forty minutes by car from home. Every morning, I drove him to school. The class had children of different ages. The teacher treated Leland with love and always had a way for Leland to sit in the class at ease.

All was well until one day we were on our way to school as usual. When we were close to school, we suddenly heard an explosive sound. At first, I thought someone had set off firecrackers, but after a couple of minutes, police cars and ambulances were racing toward the school's location and I realized there was a gunfight between gangs like ones in the movies. Somebody got shot and died on the spot. I was so terrified! Bullets don't have eyes. If the shooting had been one minute later, Leland and I could have died on the street.

Leland was sleeping in the car, so he didn't know about the gunfight, but I knew it was time to leave. Can I really find schools with loving teachers who have patience and perseverance to help Leland during his schooling years?

Although I was filled with worries and insecurities, I always believed there must be a school that was a good fit for Leland and a teacher to help him learn.

# Hidden talents unleashed

Throughout the years, I would have Leland try anything deemed by experts to have benefits for autistic children. I am tenacious, action-oriented and persistent. I would remove all obstacles to find ways for Leland to have opportunities to learn. Since the day Leland was diagnosed with autism, I tirelessly gathered information and sought public resources and programs.

When I learned the government offered a horseback-riding therapy program for autistic children, I immediately registered Leland. Even though the waiting period was a year, it was well worth the wait. Among all the trainings Leland had received, horseback riding and swimming gave him immeasurable help. Both sports unleashed his athletic potential and talent. Leland became a competitive swimmer who participated in numerous swim meets.

Leland started to learn riding at the age of five. Once a week, I drove him to a horse ranch that was an hour away. The course didn't start with riding because it was a progressive program. In the beginning, to help conquer their fear of big horses, children stood on the horses' backs with teachers' assistance. The teachers would conduct a set of exercises to practice balancing and to get used to riding motions. Leland learned new vocabularies and how to follow instructions in a repetitive way – very beneficial to him. During the whole training process, there were at least three teachers for each student to help them learn and to minimize risks.

Horseback riding made me realize that for children, especially those overly sensitive children, no matter whether the activity was riding or something new, as long as the initial experience was positive, they wouldn't be scared and were willing to continue. Leland rode for thirteen years, rain or shine and became friends with the horses. He progressed from a beginner to participating in competitions. Leland did countless sketches and paintings of horses and cowboys. Some are self-portraits of him riding horses or just being with the horses.

After returning to Taiwan, I continued taking him to horse ranches from time to time to practice until 2012, when he fell from a horse. I wasn't there so I couldn't recreate the situation to help him get rid of his fear. He still refuses to go on horseback. It is still a mystery today. Swimming is another story.

Leland was afraid of water. Every day when he took a shower, he wouldn't stop crying. I knew nothing about "touch sensitivity." I thought he simply didn't like show-ers and that his aversion might get milder with time. When Leland was 3-4 years old, we met Temple Grandin, who told me that she lived on the east coast, where it rains a lot.

"For me, the sound of rain is as shocking as the sound of a machine gun. When the raindrops hit on my face, it feels like needles pricking on my face."

When I learned that, I was petrified and couldn't utter a word! Water coming out of the shower hitting Leland's body was like bullets or needles pricking him. He was in pain but couldn't express it to me, so the daily shower was torturous for him. This guilt will always remain with me.

After changing from showers to baths, Leland became less afraid of water. Furthermore, I took him to the community swimming pool. The first time, he was afraid of getting his face wet and held onto me tightly. I knew he didn't like to have his head and face wet. I tied a dry towel on my head and as soon as his head or face was wet, I would wipe him off. I repeatedly wiped him, then tied the towel back onto my head until he finally adjusted to his head and face being wet. Little by little he was able to put his head in the water.

Jason was talented in swimming. When Leland was four years old, his brother could already swim very well and was picked to be on his school's swim team.

When Leland was no longer afraid of having his head and face wet, I felt it was time for swimming lessons, so I asked the swim coach to teach him. My original intent was for Leland to learn to swim and be able to save himself when needed. That's all. The coach looked at skinny little Leland and said, "Come back next year."

I kept taking Leland to the swimming pool to play in the water. When the next year arrived, I again asked the coach to teach him. He looked at the little boy who hadn't gained any weight or grown an inch and said, "Come back next year." After "next year" and the "next year," I still kept asking the coach and continued taking Leland to the pool with his brother. One day, the coach unexpectedly walked over to us and asked Leland, "Do you want to learn with your brother? We can give it a try."

I figured the coach was either touched by my persistence or the timing was right. After all, Leland was almost nine years old and we waited for three years.

The beginning of swimming lessons wasn't smooth. I had to stay by the pool to "translate" the coach's instructions and be there as a cheerleader. To ease the tension, I made a joke with the coach. "Hey! Leland might be swimming in the first lane one day!" He replied bluntly, "Don't even think about it. Don't dream the impossible."

I didn't want Leland to paint around the clock. There must be some additional potential in Leland that we hadn't discovered. Therefore, to discover his potential, I let him try everything. Besides going to school, he had horseback riding class once a week and swimming lessons 2-3 times a week. From a non-swimmer to swimming surprisingly well as time went by, the coach was shocked by Leland's improvements and decided to intensify the training. Once Leland started his special training, he swam even faster than his brother. Leland was always the fastest swimmer in community swim meets.

Leland not only swam fast but could swim for a long time. Once he started to swim, he could continue for two hours. The coach therefore suggested that he join the school team. I accompanied Leland to the swim team's trial, where he passed with ease. Leland was ten years old that year.

I don't recall the details of how Leland learned to swim and how he could swim so fast. I only remember that he practiced day after day, year after year. Suddenly, one day, he swam like a fish. Everything changed since; he had grown taller and gained weight, becoming handsome. Before that, his height and weight had been the same for a long time and he had appeared to be fragile.

*Soccer team, 1996.*

After joining the swim team, he started to represent his school in swim meets all over the state. He once earned a 100-meter medal from a competition in San Francisco and he represented Los Angeles in other events. It seemed as if everyone noticed Leland and saw the transformation in him.

Leland's thought process is not complex. When he had a competition approaching, he wasn't nervous at all. He was excited and happy to be in a competition every time, simply because he won medals and enjoyed pizzas afterward. He was already a well-known artist at that time, but the rewards from winning when swimming were more immediate and direct than painting.

Even though he wasn't nervous, I was stressed! Every time he was in a relay race, I became more stressed. He had to practice over and over before a race. I worried, imagining scenarios where he didn't understand the rules, or didn't catch the baton well, or was in a daze, or had unstable emotions. I worried about anything that would affect the team. The attitude of some American mothers was "We must win." If we lost, they tended to blame

Leland for impacting the team's performance. I didn't want Leland to miss out on race participation, so we spent an enormous amount of practice time preparing for a race that lasted only a few minutes.

Leland still swims often. Every time I see him in the water, I think to myself, this is his learning pattern and his natural talent. Once he gets used to a rhythm of patterns, he can go on forever. Swimming is comprised of repetitive patterns, in which he doesn't have to be mindful of anything except to keep swimming till the end. If he was not given an end, I figured that he would keep swimming till he has no more energy. Sometimes, I can't help wondering whether or not Kua Fu, the Chinese mythical character who thought he was invincible and chased the sun tirelessly, also had autism.

Before swimming, Leland had been wearing the same size pants for 3–4 years without any growth, as if his life had stopped and never gone forward, as if the Goddess of Growth had abandoned him in the wild. But once he began swimming, he grew taller and became more handsome.

Shooting basketballs and bowling have similar effects. As long as Leland gets the angle correct and has enough strength, the ball can go into the basket or strike all of the bowling pins. Repeated practice of repetitive movements created "muscle memory." Swoosh! Swoosh! Kathunk! Kathunk! He can stand at the same spot and keep throwing balls into the basket or striking every single pin.

However, he can't join a basketball team because he can never learn team play and how to cooperate or follow complicated rules. He would probably throw the ball into the other team's basket or keep breaking rules. If he was in a game, he probably would foul out quickly and have to leave the game. In addition, he would be blamed by his teammates and their parents.

# An artistic genius

After drifting from one school to another for three years, we finally found a home in Barbara's class. There were eight students with different disabilities between 5-13 years old. There were also three teaching assistants. When Leland enrolled, he was almost six years old.

In the beginning I accompanied Leland, but it's not common to see a mother so attached to a child in the U.S. Usually the parents trust the school and teachers. Putting trust aside, I wanted to be in 100% control of Leland's conditions so I could help him learn more effectively.

Barbara looked at me and said, "I've never met a mother like you." I didn't know if that was a compliment or a different way to say, "You're driving me crazy!"

I told her determinedly, "My child must get a good education. I want to give him a learning environment and opportunities equal to what his older brother has. I will take him anywhere to learn as long as he can improve." I added that if it takes going to outer space with Leland to learn, I would do it!

At that time, Leland wanted to draw nonstop. To distract his attention and to broaden his life experience, I took him for horseback riding, swimming and gymnastics. During school holidays, our whole family would go on trips. When Jason joined the Boy Scouts, we went camping, sold chocolates at supermarkets to raise money, paid our respects at a veterans' cemetery on Veteran's Day and went to the beach to pick up trash. We joined practically every activity.

Every summer, my sister-in-law Chun-Yan would bring her three sons to attend summer programs in the U.S. and stay with us. Therefore, there were at least 5-9 kids playing at home during the summer. When there was no activity, I would arrange play dates, inviting neighborhood kids and Jason's classmates. The main incentive was the cake and the pizza I baked. Growing up in Café Astoria, I was good at baking.

The challenge was to keep the kids busy. Through playing I wanted Leland to interact with others and learn to take turns. Of course, I wanted those little guests to have fun so they would want to come again. Actually, they just wanted to come for the snacks!

*A bookstore in Los Angeles displaying Leland's artworks in its window.*

Not only did this social training make Leland less afraid of being amongst strangers, he actually enjoys a boisterous atmosphere with a group of people and always looks at them with a smile. He is there but not really there, he is at ease and happy. Little did I know that later in life he would be presented to large audiences on various international platforms.

The reason why I tried so hard to fill up Leland's schedule was to discourage him from drawing constantly. I wanted him to be like other children, running around, watching cartoons, telling jokes, playing with friends and cousins, getting so excited to tell his mom about what happened in school, making up stories, telling a little lie, not wanting to come home sometimes, or preferring to stay with friends. I even stubbornly assumed that if I took away his paintbrushes, he might gradually become a normal child - as long as I made a great effort.

By my traditional thinking, there should be a "normal" path in life. Being a human being, the ultimate goal is to be self-sufficient, to live independently, with no need to rely on others but able to cooperate with people and integrate into society at the same time. If a person can't achieve this goal, it's because he or she doesn't work hard enough.

Therefore, when Leland was four years old, I made up my mind to take away his pen and paper and didn't allow him to draw. Since he couldn't draw on paper, he drew with his finger in the air, as if anything could be his canvas. One day, Barbara received a gift from Leland, a painting of a classroom scene from his previous class.

After observing Leland for a while, she appreciated this child who painted all the time. To her, Leland was a gem. Barbara noticed that although Leland couldn't express himself like a "normal" person, he was capable of receiving signals. He had feelings for what he experienced. He didn't communicate with language but with painting. "Leland has an innate talent in painting," she told me seriously. "Please don't stop him. Don't kill this precious gift."

What I saw in Leland was a child who could not stop drawing. No matter what he drew or how well he drew, all I saw was a compulsive be-havior – which made me crazy! I wanted him to stop and alter his behavior. However, Barbara saw a different Leland: she could tell immediately that his paintings were magical and unique, arising from natural talent. She said natural talent can't be hidden, shouldn't be oppressed. I knew Leland would keep on drawing if I didn't direct him to do other activities.

When Barbara suggested that I take Leland to get a talent assessment in arts at the University of California, I had never before heard of such an assessment. I wondered how an assessment was possible for a child who couldn't talk.

The process of the assessment was much more complicated than I had anticipated. I thought we simply had to submit a few paintings to the experts. It turned out that reviewing paintings was just the first step. We had to go there to be tested in person in order to prove that Leland's work was genuine. For seven days in succession, I drove him to the exam venue. I asked the staff if, given the fact that he had autism, I could accompany Leland, but my request wasn't approved. Each time Leland walked into the classroom by himself, I prayed.

The assessment was to observe Leland drawing a series of paintings. Every day, he was given a different topic, using different media. I guess it was a piece of cake for Leland; after all, that was exactly what he did every day! To my surprise, after seven days he was authenticated as a genius in arts. I said, "But he has autism!" The authorities said they only determined if he had artistic talent and did not evaluate whether or not he was autistic.

After receiving the genius in art status, I took Leland and a bunch of art geniuses to attend courses at the University of California every Saturday for ten years. The courses were diverse, including sketching, oil painting, floriculture and clay pottery.

In addition to classroom courses, there were weekly field trips to museums, gardens, parks, etc. to see, smell, touch and paint in real time.

Leland enjoyed attending courses with a big group of people. He was curious about what other people were drawing. One time the class assignment was to imitate a black and white picture using only the left hand; that's when I realized Leland could also draw with his left hand. Everyone handed in the required black and white painting – except Leland. His work was in color.

During those ten years, Leland had exposures to different teachers and artistic styles. We visited every art museum in Los Angeles and saw countless exhibitions. Leland's diversified artwork can be attributed to the training and the enriched program he was in during that period of time.

If Leland could fully express himself, the question I want to ask the most is, "How do you decide the colors in your painting? Red giraffes, yellow feet, green sky. What makes you draw so freely and in such an unrestrained way?"

In the U.S. there is no gifted class at the national level. The program Leland attended was directed by the state universities to find those talented "seedlings" and cultivate them. The course is probably the equivalent to the gifted class of arts program in Taiwan. Leland's classmates varied from elementary school students to college students – but only he had autism.

Every week I was there as his studying buddy, phrasing instructions from the teacher in ways he could understand. Apart from attending classes, there were also countless art museums to visit. After a few years, I think I'm the person who benefited the most. I felt as if I had earned several college-level credits in the arts!

Leland developed a habit of buying art catalogs after seeing an exhibition. He would read them carefully after getting home. I didn't know how much he understood but he probably had learned something. When visiting an art gallery or museum, Leland would read all the displayed information and follow an audio guide if available. I've never seen such a hard-working student!

A signature behavior of autism is stubbornness. However, there are no boundaries in Leland's paintings: they can be color or black and white. The topics and painting media are diverse, based on his life experience at the time. He could paint on driftwood, on plain pottery, or even paint over an old painting, turning it into a new piece of work. Why? The answer could be that Leland was at a fresh starting point every time he painted, influenced by innumerable exhibits he had seen with his art class, the many art catalogs he had read, and frequent traveling.

Leland's paintings often represented his school in competitions and won countless prizes. But he doesn't react to fame. He would never understand why anyone gets so excited and proud when one of his paintings is chosen to be included in a museum's art collection. He only knew that his paintings were displayed everywhere.

*The billboard at Westwood Charter School, where Leland was Artist of the Year, displaying his version of Picasso's Girl Before the Mirror.*

Jason was constantly asked by his classmates' parents: "Leland is your brother? He paints so well!" Jason received a lot of praise for his brother. Since his brother was quite famous in school, Jason's identity had been upgraded to "Leland's brother." As a child, Jason was embarrassed by Leland's disability. But after Leland was recognized as a savant artist, Jason has been very proud and supportive of his younger brother.

In the meantime, I was still finding opportunities to push Leland beyond painting. At thirteen years old, when his first art exhibit opened, I finally convinced myself not to struggle anymore and accepted Leland's fate. Painting was his destiny and I will be there with him all the way.

*Moose Cattlemen in 101, 2010, 51" x 35", acrylic on canvas.*

# A gem was under my nose

We have met Temple Grandin a few times, each time with life-changing impact. Dr. Grandin is a professor of animal science, an inventor, a consultant to the livestock industry, an author, the subject of an Emmy and Golden Globe-winning documentary, the subject of an HBO biopic, a spokesperson about autism and one of Time magazine's most influential people in the world. She has transformed both Leland's and my life in unimaginable ways.

Temple is a legendary figure for autistic patients. Since their inner world had been a closed door, Temple was the person who opened it for us. She not only opened the door but also showed everything to us, like a doctor operating with precision, giving us insight into that inner world. "Look! This is how we feel and this is how we think."

If I hadn't met Temple Grandin, I think I would still prohibit Leland from painting. Despite his being authenticated as an art genius, I wanted him to "be" a normal person rather than a savant artist.

The first time I met Temple, Leland was five years old. She was already a Doctor in Animal Science and was invited to give a speech by the California Autism Foundation. The school spread the news to parents with autistic children. For me, that was certainly a chance in a lifetime. I went to the speech with a boatload of questions.

At that time, my life was in chaos. I couldn't get enough information regarding autism, I couldn't find the correct school and I was at odds with my family. After the speech, I stood in line for a long time for a chance to ask my questions.

When I finally met her in person, my impression was that she was reserved, not approachable. When I spoke, she avoided eye contact with me. I was so desperate, like a person trying to grab a drifting piece of wood in the ocean, I thought she wasn't listening. I kept moving in the direction she was looking to make sure she saw me and heard me. When I moved, she would look the other way. Although I kept moving to the right and to the left, our eyes never crossed.

Leland doesn't look at the eyes of the person he is talking to either; this is a common trait of autism. I was so flustered that I only saw her as an expert and forgot that she has autism as well.

When Leland was thirteen years old, I saw her again. He had just shown his first art exhibition and was recognized as a genius in art. However, I was the only one who didn't accept this fact.

"I don't want him to paint nonstop. I want him to be a normal person. How can I help him?" I asked Temple.

"What's your definition of 'normal'?" she asked. She replied to me word by word while looking the other way. "Don't put too much emphasis on his behavior because he will always be like this. I am the same. There are still a lot of things I can't conquer and I am in my fifties."

*He will always be like this.* What Temple said was the fact that I refused to accept. I didn't say anything and she continued, "Don't put all your attention on his disability. You have to focus on his ability. Let him develop what he is good at would be the best help." Her words were like a slap on my face and opened my blind spot. I had always wanted to change Leland and cure his illness. I was so sure that I could cure his illness. I was almost like a maniac, not knowing what can be changed, what cannot be; what should be changed versus not. My efforts were to let Leland try everything "normal" children were capable of. Even if he couldn't learn something well, as long as he learned one more word, went to one more concert, conversed a little more with a friend, I was happy.

However, I forgot to look at what he is good at. I forgot to appreciate and read into his paintings. More importantly, I forgot to learn, to interpret the message Leland is expressing with colors and patterns. It's like a gem was right in front of me, but I blindly ignored it. Thanks to Temple Grandin, it was not too late for me to come around and to cherish this beautiful gem.

# What Temple Grandin has taught us

Temple Grandin has probably published the most books by any autistic author in the world. Over a third of livestock facilities in the U.S. are designed by her.

Apart from her biography "Emergence: Labeled Autistic," she has eight or nine additional books about autism and animal behaviors. Two of her books have been translated into Chinese: "Thinking in Pictures: My Life with Autism" and "The Way I See It: A Personal Look at Autism and Asperger's."

Compared to "normal people," autistic patients are usually referred to as "children from the outer space," "children of the stars," "little shells," "deep blue kids," "sky walkers." But all those embellished labels still mean communication obstacles exist. No outsiders can enter their mysterious inner universes.

But from Sigmund Freud's point of view, no one is really "normal." Neural science also proves that when one part of talent is overdeveloped it's probably due to the deficiency of another part. There is a school of thought that a person with autism and extraordinary talent in painting or in math can lose the special talent gradually when social and communication skills become more "normal." As far as I'm concerned, Temple is a God-sent angel to help people learn about autism.

She was diagnosed with autism at the age of fifteen. Autistic symptoms usually show up between 12-24 months. Leland was the same. When a baby starts to resist holding by pushing away or screaming, that may be a sign. Temple was a baby who resisted being held but could stay quietly in the stroller. "Since I can remember, I dislike other people hugging me. I do want to experience the good feeling of being hugged, but when people hug me, too much stimuli wash over me like a tidal wave. I then fight to get away like a trapped wild animal."

Temple wasn't talking at age three. Her mother, a journalist, realized that this child had problems. Besides not talking, she didn't look people in the eyes, she cried a lot, she didn't have interest in people, she was constantly in a daze - all typical autistic symptoms. After taking an auditory test, her hearing was confirmed to be normal. A neurologist concluded that she had brain damage. At that time, most doctors didn't know about

*Left to right: Jason, Leland, Dr. Temple Grandin, and Karen at the 2014 Training the Talent of Artists with Autism exhibit.*

autism; children who had trouble with their emotions were usually given similar diagnoses.

Many experts suggested that Temple be hospitalized to receive treatment. Her mother followed the neurologist's suggestion and found a kindergarten which provided language therapy for Temple. There were two teachers taking care of six children. When Temple was in junior high school, she was expelled because she threw textbooks at her classmates. Her mother found a boarding school where Temple met Mr. William Carlock, a science teacher who had worked for NASA. He became her mentor and helped significantly toward building up her self-confidence. He used different teaching materials to inspire Temple and she understood she had to study hard to get into a university.

Temple remembers the frustration she felt when she was three years old and couldn't talk. "I understood things people said to me, but I just couldn't say what I wanted to say." Apart from losing her temper and screaming, she didn't know how to communicate. Once she lost control and bit a teacher's leg.

Her mother knew how to deal with her. She told the teachers that when Temple loses her temper, the best response was for the teachers to stay calm. Shouting would only make her more hysterical. But when Temple went home she would be punished. For example, no TV for the entire day. Punishment was necessary. Temple learned she couldn't do whatever she liked. The discipline in school and at home were coordinated; Temple's mother and the teachers were all on the same page.

"I used to scoop up a handful of sand and let it go through my fingers frequently. I would stare at it and look at every grain of sand flowing past my fingers like a scientist observing something through the microscope. When I did that, I could shut the outside world off." That was the way Temple calmed herself down. But she also knew if she did nothing but play with the sand all day long, she wouldn't learn and make progress. Therefore, "young autistic children need to have well-planned daily routines, no matter in school or at home." I believe I've fulfilled a mother's duty regarding this point.

In addition to the sense of touch, autistic patients are usually oversensitive to sounds. When there's too much noise, Temple would shut the world off by shaking or spinning.

Normal children can connect language to things in daily life naturally, but autistic children cannot. The way to teach them language varies from person to person. One type of child may appear to be deaf before two years old, but may understand language at age three. Temple belongs to this type: she could understand words adults said to her; however, when adults talked to each other, the sounds would be meaningless to her. The other type of child appears to be normal but doesn't talk at age 1 ½-2 years. Their sensory system becomes confused and they can't deal with or understand things and sounds around them, so they just seal themselves off.

People without autism can hardly understand how it feels to have "confused senses." Temple gave an example: "If the teacher grabs my chin and forces me to look at her, I would shut down my ears." And this is a description from a person with high-functioning autism. She just can't look and listen at the same time or quickly switch her attention between two different stimuli. Another autistic patient says that he can't look into people's eyes because eyeballs are constantly moving, which is unbearable.

*Nighttime Giraffes*

What Temple Grandin wants to tell us is that many behaviors of autistic patients might seem bizarre, but they are actually reactions triggered by over-intensive senses. The circuit is overloaded so they scream out of fear. "Even now, people whistling in the middle of the night can make my heart-beat accelerate." Autistic people have to study in a quiet environment with no flickering fluorescent lights and no disturbances.

There's another question: Do autistic patients have feelings? Temple said, "Rationally, I know a sunset is beautiful but I can't feel it."

Autistic patients don't understand the complicated emotions in interpersonal relationships. They only understand a few simple emotions, such as fear, anger, happiness, sadness. Temple explains, "I can't experience some emotions."

The first time Temple noticed her feelings were different from other people was when she was in high school. Her roommate had a crush on their physics teacher but she couldn't understand that sentiment. "As far as I'm concerned, every proper social behavior needed to be acquired by intelligence. My social skills have become more polished as I gained more life experiences."

That is why I must expose Leland to the outside world, to travel, to make more contacts with people. I don't want him to stay at home and paint all the time.

*Zebras, 2009, 46" x 31", acrylic on canvas.*

Regarding obstinate behavior of autistic children, Temple thinks that we should not stop it but help develop it into constructive activities or even a career. "People pay too much attention to the disability of autistic children and neglect to develop their talents."

People frequently ask Temple why she understands cows so well and can design from "a cow's perspective." She says that she has to give the credit to autism. "The reason why I can cooperate with animals so well is mostly out of a simple fact that I see so many connections between their behaviors and some autistic behaviors."

For instance, a cow's reaction to an unexpected event is possibly similar to an autistic child's reaction to a subtle change in the environment. "Autistic children don't like anything out of order, such as a string hanging on a piece of furniture, an uneven carpet, books not neatly placed on the bookshelf; they also notice tiny changes that normal people neglect." Observing subtle alterations that "normal" people neglect is also one of Leland's traits. At an Eslite bookstore in Taipei, Leland once rearranged all the books in a bookcase.

Temple has another opinion about animals. She asked, "Is this a primitive instinct to fight against predators?" When animals are sure about a safe pasture - even if there is a good stretch of meadow four yards away - still won't go there. So when a cattleman brings the herd to a new area of grazing for the first time, he has to make sure the herd feeds everywhere in the new pasture.

What autistic children and cows have in common also includes that they both freak out with certain things. For example, a child may be putting on a blue jacket when the fire alarm bell sounds. The child therefore makes a connection between the alarm and the clothing. A frightening memory is stored as a picture, sound, smell or touch. A strong frightening memory can be suppressed but never deleted. Temple puts it in a humorous way. "Maintaining a long list of frightening memories can help animals to survive in the animal kingdom. An animal forgetting where it saw a lion last will not live long."

How do autistic patients think? There are two different ways to understand the world: visual thinking and lingual thinking.

"My brain is like an internet search engine which only picks up images," Temple said.

Most autistic patients have a better visual ability than other people, so they are good at puzzles, directions or memorizing an abundance of information with a glance. Relatively speaking, their language abilities are not so good. Even for high-functioning autistic patients, the language used can be formulaic, formal and out-of-date.

Those who use visual thinking are thinking from certain images. For example, Temple's concept of dogs is a collection of every dog she has seen. She would open an image file or a visual index storing these dogs. The more dogs she sees, the bigger the file or index becomes. In this way, knowledge is constructed – image by image.

"After accumulating over a long period, I've constructed a huge database in my memory from past experiences, television, movies and newspapers. They help me avoid possible awkward moments my autism could cause in a social circumstance." This process is another reason why we have to help autistic children to "accumulate real-life experiences."

When Temple reads, she turns words into images, even a colorful movie. Or she scans all the words into her database like a camera and reads them later. If the text can't be turned into images, such as in a philosophy book or an analysis of future cattle markets, she is not able to understand.

Her life's meaning is based on the pursuit of science and intellectuality. But how to understand abstract concepts like "peace" and "integrity?" Temple pictures them as symbolic images. For example, imagine "peace" as the scene of signing a peace treaty in the news; imagine "integrity" as putting a hand on the Bible in court. She uses the same process to understand prayers. She imagines "sin" as a black and orange billboard saying No Trespassing. As for "Amen," she can never understand why we have to say "Amen" at the end of a prayer.

All in all, Temple believes that the way she thinks is similar to how computers calculate. She can explain her thinking process, step by step. She didn't realize her pattern of thinking was different from others until she attended university. By that time, she also realized that most people relied on emotional signals.

In her books and public appearances, Temple lets people "enter" the world of autism. That world is not only filled with strange behaviors but also with surprising and incredible talents.

"If I could become normal with snaps of fingers, I wouldn't do it. Because I will not be who I am. Autism is part of how I am made." That is the line that touches me the most from Temple Grandin. As a result, I stopped pushing Leland to become "normal," because then he wouldn't be himself.

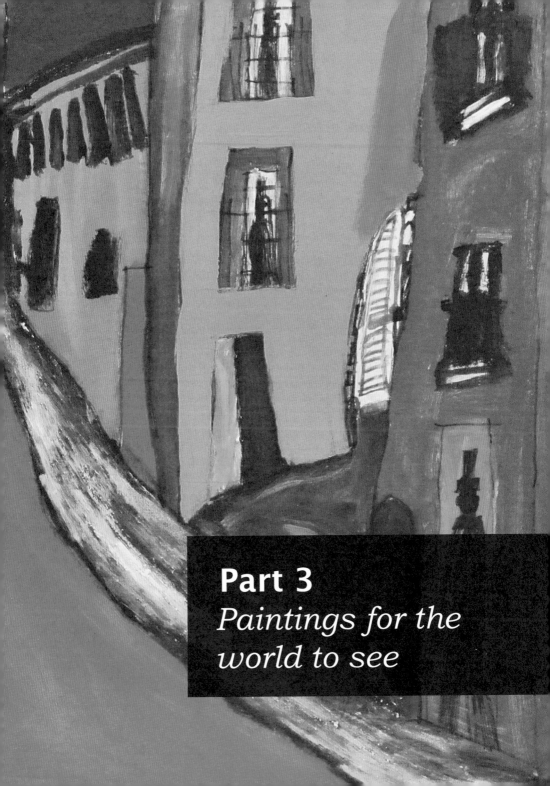

**Part 3**
*Paintings for the world to see*

# He was born an artist

My son, Leland, has autism, but he also has talents in painting as well as in sports. He is an artist who receives invitations to hold exhibitions from countries worldwide all year round. His works are collected by art museums and art collector Charles C. Y. Chen. Yet Leland has no idea he has a powerful fund-raising appeal.

My son has autism, yet he was chosen as one of Taiwan's 10 Outstanding Young Persons in 2013. When he was onstage to receive the award, attendees couldn't even tell he has autism. This honor means the world to our family but I couldn't explain to him how commendable and precious it was to receive this award.

Someone asked me, "What will Leland contribute to Taiwan after receiving this award?" I didn't know how to answer because contributing is exactly what Leland has been doing for many years. He has held countless exhibitions where visitors learned the artist behind those works is from Taiwan and named Leland Lee. Moreover, we have represented Taiwan in numerous international seminars as autistic patient and parents with a mission to raise awareness that autism is not terrible at all.

Due to the lack of understanding of autism, the majority of people thought that these kids were good for nothing. The title of 10 Outstanding Young Persons can be the message that they are not a burden but our pride and joy.

When Leland received the 10 Outstanding Young Persons award from Mr. Jin-Pyng Wang, President of the Legislative Yuan, he could not comprehend the significance of this honor. At the award ceremony, Mr. Wang said that despite having autism, Leland Lee's paintings reflect his own perspective of the world. The award is a well-deserved recognition of Leland's achievements.

Most people might label Leland as "autistic + an artist." To me, he is an artist and painting is his whole being, an artist who happens to have autism.

*Beijing Olympic, 2012, 36" x 29", acrylic on paper.*

# Conversations through paintings

Neurologist and author Oliver Sacks was instrumental in helping me understand Leland's paintings. He wrote a story called The Autistic Artist in his book, "The Man Who Mistook His Wife for a Hat."

The main character in The Autistic Artist is José, Sacks' patient. José has an eidetic or "photographic" memory. Sacks wondered if José simply copies an image he has seen to his paintings. Or does José incorporate his own creation in the process?

Sacks asked José to paint based on a scenic photo which had a canoe in the center. The result surpassed a reproduction. Every detail in the painting illustrated that José has imagination and creativity. There was not just a canoe but José's own canoe. Not only imagination and creativity were shown in José's paintings; Sacks also saw a sense of humor, a fairytale-like story and a variety of other elements.

José started to have autistic symptoms as well as epilepsy after a fever at the age of eight. Gradually, he lost his ability to talk. Schooling was stopped and he had no outside exposure for fifteen years. He was monitored tightly by his family. But José kept his passion for painting, animals and plants. Painting was the only way that he could express himself and communicate with the world.

Autistics' natural instincts are rarely influenced by the outside world. They are "doomed" to be segregated. People would see primeval characteristics if their inner world could be seen. This is one of the reasons that autism is different from schizophrenia. The latter's complaints are mostly due to influences from the outside environment, while the former can't be influenced.

People with ASD keep to themselves, in cocoons. Even though they have no "horizontal" relationships with people, society and culture, they still have close "vertical" relationships with nature and instincts. Does it make sense to interpret Leland's behaviors this way? I don't have answers. But I'm sure that even if his mind is like a closed container, it's not vacuum sealed. When I put various things in, they would stir up subtle reactions to connect Leland and the external world.

What kind of reactions? Leland chose to tell me through his paintings.

Thinking back, Leland has been telling me a lot of secrets via his paintings, beginning a long time ago.

*Jump! With Jason in an open field in southern France.*

*White water rafting: Leland (center, standing), his father, Philip (center, sitting) and brother Jason (far right, standing).*

# All the flowers smiled

When Leland was two years old, he could already draw flowers with smiley faces, like the flower prints from artist Takashi Murakami.

Leland was born in May, full of blooming flowers in late spring. We lived in a community that was covered by flowers, sunflowers, cherry blossoms, roses and daffodils. Those blooming flowers probably had the strongest visual effect on Leland.

As soon as Leland took up a paintbrush, he started to draw flowers without any guidance; he drew flowers with smiley faces nonstop. Did those flowers look like smiles to him or did Leland actually "see" the flowers smiling at him? I don't know. Anyhow, he kept drawing day after day – which drove me crazy. All of his flower paintings in total could be as thick as a book of a thousand pages.

The series with smiley faces seemed all the same. Yet with a careful eye you can see subtle differences, such as the color, the quantity and the size. The flowers aren't alone either, sometimes they are accompanied by a sun, a bird, or a school bus. There was a painting in which he had drawn a school bus and a flower. The flower was very big, while the school bus was very tiny, as if it was taken by a camera's macro lens. The flower was in the foreground, while the bus was in the background. Through a camera's lens, the background would be blurry, but in Leland's eyes, everything was completely clear and sharp, no matter if the object is far or near.

Leland liked riding on the school bus, although it took time to train him to take the bus alone. At first, I took the bus with him, then I brought him to the bus stop and drove behind the school bus. I told him I would see him getting off the bus from my car. This helped ease his mind by knowing where Mommy was and when she was going to pick him up. That was the way to let him go: little by little. I told myself, "I have to learn to let go from time to time."

On school bus rides, his eyes would still follow the flowers. Therefore, school buses and flowers kept appearing in his paintings for a while.

A long time after the days of school buses, I took Leland to an exhibition of Takashi Murakami. The collection on exhibit happened to be flowers with smiley faces. Leland had a confused look; I could see many question marks in his head! I understood what he was thinking. "Why does this person draw the same things as I do? Is he copying me? Why are my paintings here?"

*Flowers Singing "You are My Sunshine."*

# The feet that have walked a long way

When the series of flowers with smiley faces came to an end, drawings of feet followed!

When Leland was two or three years old, he started to draw feet. For the next twenty years, feet have constantly been in Leland's paintings. Many characters in his paintings have big bare feet. He even made a painting with just feet, nothing but big and small feet. Why does he care so much about feet?

Leland had difficulty with balance since he was a kid. He walked with faltering steps. I didn't understand the reason. He also doesn't like to wear shoes; they restrain his feet, which makes him feel uncomfortable. When he entered elementary school, I realized he was born with flat feet. Those who have flat feet can't walk for too long; otherwise, they often feel foot pain.

During Physical Education classes in school, Leland's feet often felt uncomfortable, so he would take off his shoes and run with bare feet. I gathered that the hurting feet constantly reminded their owner that they were in pain, so the owner in turn used paintings instead of words to say, "I know you are in pain," "I feel for you." Those painted feet are probably the dialogues between Leland and his feet.

I also noticed that the feet Leland drew were flat and straight until one day, there was an arch in the feet. Maybe it meant the relationship between him and his feet had improved?

Then, Leland started to draw moose people. The creatures in the paintings look like moose but also human – with feet like Leland's. I asked him about the feet-only drawing, "Why are there so many feet in this drawing?"

"Leland walks a lot" was his reply, which meant that the feet bring him to places. Without the feet, he wouldn't go anywhere. Indeed, he keeps walking and I keep walking along side of him. Despite pain in the feet and bumpy roads ahead filled with difficulties and challenges, we will endure and keep walking forward together.

*Feet, 2014, 20" x 24", acrylic on canvas.*

*Scream, 2001, 18" x 24", acrylic on canvas.*

# The Scream, the painting that blows everyone's mind

Picasso has to take credit for the fact that Leland is authenticated as an art genius. Leland was seven years old when an exhibition of Picasso's work came to Los Angeles I hesitated about whether or not to take Leland since tickets were US $30, which was not cheap at the time. Leland surely had no concept of money but I had to be wise with expenditures.

That was a chance of a lifetime. I convinced myself and took Leland to the exhibition. There was a sea of people in the venue. Even though no one talked loud, we were still surrounded by conversations from all sides. Leland frowned and looked uncomfortable while in the venue. I followed his pace. After what was a rather fast viewing of the exhibit, we went straight home.

Not long after the exhibition, he painted a self-portrait called The Scream. He named it himself. In the picture, Leland wears a suit, which probably comes from wearing a suit to church since he was little. The man in the suit fills the entire painting with his mouth wide open and face bright red from screaming. Self-portraits are usually considered to be a link to the creator's inner world. Picasso could be the contemporary artist with the most self-portraits. He imagined himself as different kinds of characters: a playboy, a lover, an artist, a friend, a monkey, etc.

Leland's Scream painting raised high interest among art critics. No one could believe that it was painted by a 7-year-old child. Everyone was analyzing what the child wanted to express through the painting. Is Leland like a bottomless well so deep that you can't reach? How much emotion is hidden in the well? What is Leland's painting saying?

At that time, he couldn't really talk, he could only understand some simple instructions such as "We are going to eat." But he would become confused if I said, "We are going to eat at Café Astoria later." The additional information was too much for him.

However, autism usually doesn't show externally. Leland looked very "normal." Most people would talk to him in the same way that they talk to "normal" children and wait for his response. This made him frustrated and stressed. In such a situation, he would scream. According to Temple Grandin, this behavior is called "escape by screaming." I also guessed that he was thinking, "I can't communicate fluently and can't really understand either. Please talk to me with patience. Please talk to me in the way that I can understand." The man in the suit in the painting reflects Leland himself.

Many people point out that the concept of Leland's Scream is similar to The Scream by Edvard Munch. The most important works of Munch, a Norwegian master of expressionism, are a series of paintings he called "Frieze of Life." The Scream is the most iconic among those paintings.

In the painting, there's a skeleton-like figure standing on a long bridge with his eyes wide open and hands on his face. He is screaming with his hands covering his ears against a landscape with ominous clouds in the sky. With the gloomy atmosphere and depressing colors, the whole painting seems to be spinning. It is generally thought that The Scream shows the anxiety of modern people; at the same time, there are also people who think it can represent the mental state of autistics. I am positive that Leland hadn't seen Munch's The Scream before painting his self-portrait.

Leland's self-portrait isn't as "beautiful" as his other paintings. But there's a deeper meaning behind the painting he wants to tell the world. He is actually anxious and helpless when he faces noisy sounds around him. He really wants to communicate with people – but he can't. The person in the painting stretches his arms outward as if Leland is saying "Stop! I know you're talking to me but can you listen to me and stop talking?"

Leland never explains his paintings. He actually doesn't need to explain. He uses The Scream to prove that his thinking is way more advanced than what he can express verbally. After seeing Leland's paintings, the poet Chi-Cheng Luo said, "His paintings need to be translated."

"Translating" is different from "analyzing." The former is to approach a painter's inner thoughts, while the latter is to see the artwork from an academic point of view. Sometimes, putting away complicated thinking and simply appreciating an artwork is itself an art form in learning and enjoyment.

Leland's The Scream was his first attempt to communicate his plight of living with autism and the first time people noticed his artistic talent.

*Love to Taichung, 2010, 20" x 24", acrylic on canvas.*

# His art, his universe

Dr. Susan Gao once suggested marking the date on every painting. If you lived with Leland and see what he draws every day, you would notice that he transforms whatever he sees onto papers. Dating each drawing is like dating a diary.

For instance, A Wedding Party shows the scenes from a friend's wedding that we attended in San Diego. The venue was beautifully decorated and filled with music by a live vocalist. Guests cheered and toasted the newly-weds and each other throughout the event.

Leland drew his impression of the wedding with scenes of glasses, bottles and people. I remember he wore blue clothing and the singer was dressed in khaki. But in the painting, the monotone colors became splashy ones. If you take a closer look, you can even see creases on the clothing.

No one knows how Leland decides which colors to use or why he draws in block formation. A doctor once suggested an examination of his eyes to make sure he didn't have astigmatism. The result was normal.

Not all paintings are in vibrant colors, some artworks are in black and white. One time when we were abroad, Leland had only a black pen and no colored pens were available. So he painted with the black pen, which started a black and white series of paintings.

During a different period of time, a mysterious "X" appeared in the paintings. It seemed like Leland deliberately embedded the "X" and wanted people to solve its meaning, similar to novels by Dan Brown in which the solution to conspiracy plots was often led by clues from a painting.

But Leland's paintings don't have such complexity. The "X" was his impression of windmills when we visited the Netherlands. Looking at the windmills from a distance, one sees many capital letter "X's." Also, the Eiffel Tower's structure is composed of lots of "X's." Leland can turn these simply shaped objects into detailed content. He can take "snapshots" of multiple sceneries and images and recall them from his memory to appear, all at the same time.

We had a dog named Taffy at our Los Angeles home. After Taffy passed away, Leland did a painting with five Taffy's. Each had different postures:

*Leland and his dog, Taffy.*

*Ponder, 2014, 29" x 36", acrylic on canvas.*

crouching, biting and wagging her tail. Leland recreated every posture of Taffy from memory into the composition. There was also one painting in which he drew all kinds of balls used in sports he had never played: hockey balls, baseballs, golf balls, basketballs, tennis balls. It was a big reunion of balls!

Occasionally Leland paints over an old painting. My guess is that he's not satisfied with the original and he sees a need to make changes. Or he has a new inspiration for the piece. At times when I return home from running errands, certain paintings had just disappeared. There was an awkward moment when the wife of U.S. Ambassador to Taiwan asked to see a painting of a White House limo, which was a gift from her to Leland. She knew Leland had altered the original, but I still had a hard time explaining to her. "Yes, the White House limo is still in the painting, but Leland added the Lord's prayer from the Bible on top of the original!" A more awkward incident occurred when we visited a professor at UCLA. In his office, Leland saw an old painting that had been collected by the professor. Leland went up and changed the colors on the spot!

"Why did you do that?" I asked him.

"I wanted to," he answered.

"Why this color?"

"This is the color."

People usually paint on a blank canvas. For Leland, a blank canvas or an old painting can be a new canvas. Lines and colors on an old painting don't mean it is a finished piece of work. There are way more visual images in his head than he is able to communicate.

Leland paints everything, from colors to black and white, from two-dimensional to three-dimensional, and nobody controls the content of his creations. Every time I look at Leland while he paints with earbuds in his ears, he looks focused, fearless and happy. He is in a comfort zone where he is the boss. It seems that he already knows the end result; he is just going through the motions to deliver the final version.

I believe that within Leland there is a system; every time it meets external stimulations it sparks without limitation, multiplying and dividing to expand and keep extending.

# The first art exhibition

At the age of thirteen, Leland had his first art exhibit at BGH Gallery in Santa Monica. BGH Gallery was a premiere art center that charged US $10,000 a month to rent the venue. Only top-rated artists had the opportunity to display their works there. The California Autism Foundation presented the opportunity for Leland to have an exhibition there. To me, this signifies that Leland's paintings had gained the recognition of critics.

During this first exhibition, Leland sold more than 20 paintings and we donated a portion of the profit to the California Autism Foundation. Leland has had income-earning ability since then, but he is oblivious to his earning! At his second exhibition, the price of each painting was raised to US $10,000. The pricing was assessed by professionals, not randomly set by me.

Thus began Leland's life of art exhibitions. When he was fourteen years old, we had his first exhibition in Taiwan, From Impossible to Possible, at the historic Dadaocheng Museum of Fine Arts. More than forty paintings were on display. A painting of the Taiwanese hand puppet, Door God, was collected by former Taiwan President Lee Teng Hui's foundation.

For more than twenty years, from the U.S. to Taiwan, from Taiwan to France, Venice, Vienna and China, we haven't stopped, we haven't rested. Leland raised money for Autism Academy, our church and many other charity events. In 2011, he attended Future Pass - From Asia to the World, the 54th Venice Biennale, as an artist, not as an autistic artist.

When we attended the Gifted Genius Seminars in Shanghai and Beijing, Leland was surrounded by local and international media. He was asked to appear in photos and talk about his paintings. The setting was chaotic which made me very nervous. Fortunately, Ching-Chih Kuo, Professor of Special Education of National Taiwan Normal University, and Dr. Susan Gao, Psychiatrist at National Taiwan University (NTU) Hospital, were both there and their presence helped to calm me. I am always more nervous than Leland at events. For Leland, it can't be more natural than to talk about his paintings. Painting is not only his way to get to know the world, it is also his way to respond to the world.

*Champagne Toast*        *Moose Friends Playing Sports*

In 2013, Leland was voted one of the 51st Ten Outstanding Young Persons in Taiwan. A medical institution for mental disability in Germany sent a letter to congratulate him. They also invited Leland to create the visual design for the Floral Exposition of Germany in 2014.

Due to Leland's recognition abroad, the 2014 International Symposium on Autism Spectrum Disorders was held in Taiwan with a theme on school intervention and talent development of students with ASD. Research professors from New York and Los Angeles came to the conference. Leland was like an "autism ambassador," connecting with every doctor and scholar who study autism, all with the common goal for the world to be a friendlier place to autistic children and provide more support for the parents.

## Moose, long time no see!

I clearly remember when Leland met his first moose, while the family was on a camping trip at Banff National Park in Canada. Lake Louise, the castle-like Banff Springs Hotel, Sulphur Mountain - every corner was incredibly beautiful. Leland usually wakes up early.

One day he awoke, walked outside our tent and saw several moose meandering in front of him. It was a different experience for him compared to seeing giraffes from behind a fence at the zoo! Every kid likes going to the zoo, but Leland loves to go to the zoo more than other children.

He was fascinated by the wild moose. I followed him, worrying that the moose might hurt him. I caught up with him and tried to pick him up. To my surprise, he refused. He just stood there and stared at those moose with a smile. There must have been a strong connection between him and them.

Before the camping trip ended, moose entered into Leland's art. There was a period of time where moose regularly appeared in his paintings. Amusedly, everything was a moose, every character had moose antlers. Leland decided to see this world from a moose's perspective for reasons we will never know. The world was full of moose!

"Normal" artists would think about the metaphor of "moose." They might spend a long time evaluating if they should represent moose in their paintings and might even consider the marketability of moose. They might hesitate, ponder and calculate. The opinions they have today might contradict their thoughts from yesterday.

However, for Leland, his inner voice is everything. This shows his thinking is simple and direct. The moose period ended with expanded life experience, improved motor skills and a new passion for horseback riding and swimming. The moose disappeared from Leland's paintings until he was reunited with a moose in Taiwan.

When we moved back to Taiwan, film director Zheng-Cheng Lin introduced Leland to sculptor Sho-Chi Wang at Yangming Mountain. They were working on the Twinkle Twinkle Little Stars documentary film. There was a stuffed moose head hanging in Mr. Wang's studio. Leland smiled and his eyes brightened.

He walked straight to the moose and said "Long time no see." The stuffed moose probably responded to him as well. Leland sang and talked to it; they seemed to be old friends reunited after a long time. The reunion with the moose was a big deal in Leland's life. Moose reappeared in his paintings. Interestingly, as Leland grew up, the moose did as well: they could ride a bike, hold a Mickey Mouse toy, drive a pumpkin carriage, ride a horse like a cattleman, dance, grow a mustache or wear a necktie for a banquet.

In one painting, where Leland's dear Jesus was pinned on the cross, He even had antlers on His holy head. With a closer look, one could notice the antlers had changed shape in Leland's paintings. The ones painted in the U.S. were round, while the ones painted in Taiwan were square.

In June 2009, we finished filming the documentary and went to Paris for an exhibition and vacation. Through the windows of the hotel, we could see the Eiffel Tower. We took strolls on the streets, watched people, went to see performances and visited the Louvre Museum. Leland painted scenes from Paris: an Indian man meditating on the street was transformed into a moose–man meditating and a French policeman in uniform became a moose policeman. The head of The Thinker, sculpture by Auguste Rodin, also turned into a moose head. The Eiffel Tower appeared a lot too.

The concept of imitation or duplication does not exist in Leland's brain. He observes everything, absorbs as much as he can and transfers what he sees to his paintings. The objects in paintings are created through his eyes and are like words conveying messages that Leland can't express.

Leland's painting Concert of Moose was commissioned by the Mozart School of Music in Canada. The principal, Ms. Olga Lockwood, appreciated Leland's artwork so much that she requested a painting for the school with no limitation on the theme. Leland created a painting using M–O–Z–A–R–T alphabets as the base and moose playing different instruments on top of each letter. He continues to paint with letters. He drew LOVE followed by a Bible story series and a series of Tang Dynasty poetry. Each of his paintings represents a timeline in his life and reflects his life experience at that time.

In 2011, Leland had an exclusive exhibition of Journey of Moose at the Beyond Gallery in Taipei. Moose is the most-repeated subject in his more than twenty-year painting career, his warmest friend and his craziest imagination. Just as Temple Grandin can understand cows, I believe that Leland can understand moose. There is a moose living inside his heart.

*Coffee Break*

*Russia Church, marker on paper.*

# Leland's art tells his life story

Frequently, I have been asked how many paintings has Leland produced, and I can't reply with an accurate number. Countless. There are as many paintings as there are thoughts flying across our minds.

Some people keep a diary by writing, some by photos. Other people post their feelings every hour on Facebook or Instagram. Leland uses his paintings as his diary. They are his words, his voice, his senses, his emotions, his personal record of life and expressions of his sentiments. Picasso once said that in order to leave a complete record behind, he would try his best to document his life in his paintings. In my opinion, Leland does the same; he tries his best to draw his life in paintings. They are like colorful butterflies that hatch from cocoons.

Yet, what differs Leland from Picasso is that Leland's drive comes from instinct, while Picasso had a never-ending desire to be innovative. Picasso knew he was on the leading edge, stirring up the art world.

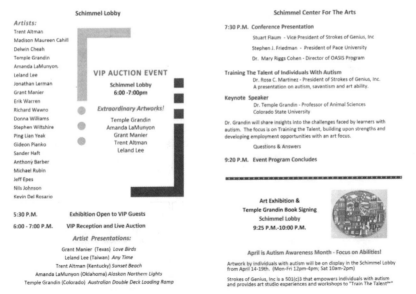

*2014 Training the Talent of Artists with Autism art exhibit and V.I.P. auction program.*

For Leland, I provide context to his life story. I try my best to give him as much life and as many visual experiences as possible. In addition to traveling, we attended classes at Taipei National University of the Arts, National Taiwan University of Arts and the special education center of National Taiwan Normal University.

We go to concerts and see performing arts at the National Theater and National Concert Hall. We see flowers at Yangmingshan National Park, did hang gliding in Wan-Li, sent paper lanterns with written wishes into the sky in Ping-Xi, visited the tea garden in Ping-Lin, viewed old wells and terraced rice fields in San-Xia, made straw scarecrows with Teacher Huang Chunming in Yilan, and had a feast at a street banquet, etc.

Mr. & Mrs. Tai-Sheng Lin, Founders of les enphants, a famous children's clothing company in Taiwan took Leland and me to experience various kinds of Taiwanese culture. Warm friendships with them as well as many others contributed to enrich life experiences that became elements in his paintings.

Every day, I deposit something new into Leland's brain. Even though I never know if it will take root and grow, I am like a farmer sowing, spreading seeds all the time. Every time Leland is attracted to a new object, he would draw it nonstop until he gets bored or the attraction is replaced by a "new love."

Streetlights in Paris, the Kremlin in Moscow, the paper lanterns of Ping-Xi, the planet Saturn, Taipei 101 (the tallest skyscraper in Taiwan) – all have come and gone. Certain objects would pop up every once in a while, such as street scenery, cowboys, horses, moose, feet, stars, the word "Any Time", and his beloved dog Taffy. The September 11 attack in New York City was in his paintings for a while.

Painting is never a chore for Leland, he never gets tired of it. For "normal" people like us, the best way to get rid of fatigue is probably by drinking a cup of tea or coffee, taking a nap or hot bath, or getting a massage. But for Leland, the best way to relax is to paint. He does the same at home or when he travels: he paints when he gets home or back to the hotel. Many writers and painters say they need inspiration to create, but it seems as if Leland never has a moment that he can't paint something. This strong energy, yearning to communicate, amazes me all the time. Leland's paintings are equal to his life story and his being.

*Any Time Gallop, 2014, 36" x 29", acrylic on canvas.*

# Any Time

I had been wondering when the words "Any Time" appeared in Leland's paintings. Was there a special story? Then I realized the answer is actually quite simple. When we lived in the U.S., whenever we arrived at a destination, I would take Leland out of the car and check the parking rule sign to see if I could park there. When I saw "No Parking" I would shake my head and read it out loud to teach Leland those words and tell him that we couldn't park there. Sometimes we would see a sign with "No Parking Any Time" on it. I told Leland, "Look, it means no parking here any minute or any second."

At any time, I talk to Leland – regardless of whether or not he understands. Any time, I am like a news feed: In simple terms, I tell him everything that I see and hear. When Leland was younger, there would be no response from him, so I fully appreciate the saying "talking to a wall!" But I diligently put in the efforts without expectation. I keep on talking. I believe that as long as I talk to him and teach him repeatedly, he can learn. Even a tiny bit would be worthwhile. I would never give up because he has severe autism. I believe that he has the potential to learn – at any time.

I fell in love with these two words, Any Time. They frequently come up in our conversations. I told Leland, "You can pray any time." I also told Jason, "You can pray any time." Even when Mommy is not around, you can still pray any time. We have to put in our best efforts any time, we have to face the light and leave the darkness any time. I will love them any time and pray for them any time. I am grateful any time.

Therefore, "Any Time" gradually entered Leland's paintings, just like oxygen and breathing, so natural that they never are the main subject in a painting. They're just embedded in a corner that brings amusement to the viewers. "Any Time" is more like Leland's signature than an object in the painting.

"Any Time" seems to be the way Leland is conveying "any time I am painting," "any time I have something to say."

In Leland's eyes, everyday people and scenes of ordinary, daily life are special subjects and worth capturing in his art.

"Any Time" has entered multiple exhibition venues and become a part of the fabric that make up Leland's view. If Leland could articulate, I think he would answer me in this way, "Art? I'm not creating art for the sake of art. I don't know what art is. I just transfer what I like onto paintings."

# One-of-a-kind Dolphin and Butterfly

I often joke that Dolphin and Butterfly is the visitor attraction at my home, occupying an entire wall. It is hard for visitors not paying attention to this painting and they usually ask shyly to take photos with the painting and the artist. This interest is also why I am not ready to part with the artwork. Many art museums want to acquire it and an art collector even wishes to place an order for Leland to paint another one. But how is it possible for him to reproduce Dolphin and Butterfly? Timing and mood changes every second for artists. Therefore, every single painting is a "one and only." Some are more precious than others because memories and emotions are woven into the painting.

Since Leland was a little kid, I have frequently taken him to a beach twenty minutes away by car. We always wait to see dolphins jumping above the water. We also watch seagulls eating dinner, or a flock of seagulls working together to fish so every seagull gets to eat. That's such a perfect scene I never get tired of watching them! Leland likes the ocean even more after he became a strong swimmer, watching sunset coloring the horizon with shades of red while waiting for the dolphins to leap above the water. There are many snapshots like that in our memory banks.

After moving to Taiwan, we still go to our home in the U.S. once a year. We like to go to the Getty Museum in Los Angeles to see exhibits and dine at a restaurant nearby. We usually choose outdoor seating to breathe the clear and salty air and take in the scenery.

During the Taipei International Floral Exposition, the whole venue became Leland's playground. He pointed at some flowers and said, "Butterflies!" He closely studied every species of flower and followed the paths of butterflies. I figured the flowers must have been smiling at him. Leland probably stored the images of flowers swinging in the wind, butterflies dancing from the exposition and sights from the beach in Los Angeles in the same folder in his memory bank.

*Preceding page:*
*Dolphin and Butterfly, 2019, 76" x 51", acrylic on canvas.*

From dolphins in the distance, plus the impressions of the floral ex-position, Dolphin and Butterfly was born. The reason why the painting is breathtaking, besides the large size, is that in reality a butterfly is only a fraction the size of a dolphin, whereas in Leland's painting the butterfly became equal in size and a good friend of the dolphin. His imagination is full of amazement and creativity!

When Leland was seventeen years old, he and I moved from the U.S. back to Taiwan. The first landmark he recognized certainly was Café Astoria. Whenever we are in Taiwan, we work at Café Astoria every day. He has learned to fold pastry boxes. He does it fast, with precision; no one can beat him. He also takes conversation and guitar lessons at the café. Leland's paintings adorn the walls on the third floor.

Café Astoria is his second home, so it is natural that the café is in his paintings. One of the Café Astoria paintings is delightful: a pink front door is paired with a bright yellow wall! Aside from mother nature, not many painters would be so bold with color choices like those. I see Café Astoria's splendor from Leland's eyes. I think this is the reason a friend once said that after you see Leland's paintings, it's hard to forget them.

The second landmark Leland recognized was Taipei 101, which can be seen from every corner in of the city due to its height of 101 stories. Leland was instantly attracted to the skyscraper and painted it frequently from every angle. On a New Year's Eve, we went to Elephant Mountain to watch the famous Taipei 101 fireworks and the building was captured in one of his paintings.

In the Taipei 101 series, there is a special piece where he used white lines against a black base to outline a foreign grandfather reading on a chair with the building in the background. Apparently, Taipei 101 and reading are connected.

Another painting of Taipei 101 is "Taipei 101 and a cow." One time we went to a mountain close to Taipei 101 and saw a cow there. Leland was almost within reach of the animal, face-to-face with the cow with Taipei 101 in the distance, therefore in that painting, the cow is very big while Taipei 101 is tiny.

Frequently, I'm speechless by Leland's great creativity. However, his imagination is actually based on real life, which we are so used to and often neglect. Leland puts together the details that we neglect, adds sugar, blends in spices, mixes in colors, and then the ingredients become the totality we call "painting" or "art.

*Dream of 101, 2014, 50" x 38", acrylic on canvas.*

*Spring Any Time, 2013, 36" x 29", acrylic on canvas.*

# Whose paintings do you like the best?

Some say that artists are narcissists, that they think they are the center of the universe and the rest of us revolve around them. They think everyone looks up to them with admiration.

Leland has seen countless art exhibitions and art catalogs since he was seven years old. From classic to modern, from avant-garde to installation art, using a multitude of media: acrylic, oils, glass, gold, silver, cooper, iron and wood. Rembrandt, Giotto, Cézanne, Van Gogh, Gauguin, Picasso, Braque, Milo, Matisse, Monet, Modigliani, Klimt and Dali.

As soon as Leland looks at a painting, he can immediately tell you who the artist is.

I know he likes Van Gogh. We even traveled to Provence so he could see the ancient Roman ruins in person and breathe the air that Van Gogh had breathed. After seeing so many works from those great artists, I was curious about which one left him with the deepest impression.

"Whose paintings do you like the best?" I once asked Leland.

He didn't even have to think twice and quickly answered, "I like Leland's the best."

I couldn't help smiling.

# Part 4
## *Lessons Leland taught me*

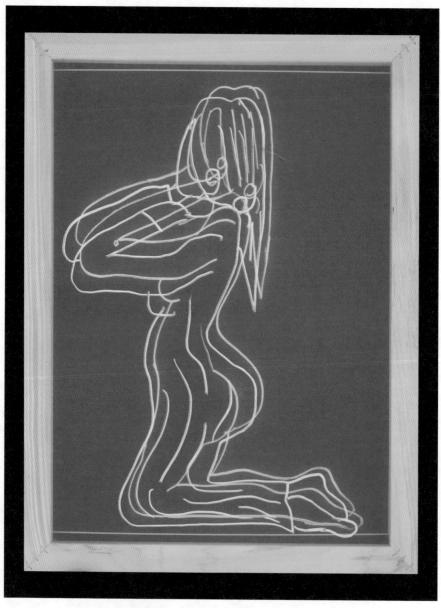

*My Fair Lady, 2012, 21" x 16", acrylic, silk and cardboard.*

# Growing up together

As autistic kids get older, hyperactivity, screaming, self-mutilation and inappropriate physical actions become more powerful; at the same time, the judgmental looks from outsiders increase as well. Mothers tolerate misbehavior, or attempt to stop their kids' improper actions, or feel ashamed by the critical stares of "How did you teach your child?"

Once I read a story on the Internet, "How to deal with a misbehaved, screaming child on the subway."

On a social networking website, a mother with an autistic child asked, "How do I deal with the public's disgusted faces and frighten looks?" Another mother answered, "It has been a long and difficult road for me from tolerating to fully accepting. If I don't accept my own child, how is it possible for family members or other people to understand and accept the child?" "Abnormal" behaviors of autistic children are realities that can't be hidden.

This mother recognized that she needed to make changes. When her child couldn't keep from screaming on an outing, she would make a gesture to let the child know that he had to be quiet. And then she would hug him lightly and compliment him by saying, "You are amazing! You have been putting up with this for so long. Hang in there! We are almost home. You are doing great! We are almost there. Mommy is here for you. We can do it!"

The mother added, "I can't stop the rude looks from the public, but I choose to put my wounded feelings on the side because I know that my child doesn't do it on purpose. I acknowledge his behaviors to clearly let people know my child is different."

When the mother's attitude changed, the reactions of others changed as well. Ever since she stopped scolding her child on the subway, ignoring people's stares and lovingly encouraging her child verbally, she felt support and understanding from the people around her. They would even come up to her child to say hello. Some people approached them on purpose to cheer for her: "Mommy! Go! Go! Go!"

Mothers have to grow up with their children and one of the definitions of growing is changing and making progress: going from not being able to comprehend to comprehension, from not being able to accept to acceptance, from seeing only negatives to seeing something positive developed from badness. Before Leland, I lived a generally carefree and comfortable life. With Leland, I have slowly transformed myself into a mother who is tough and strong, but also gentle, accepting and positive.

*Leland at work in Café Astoria.*

The first lesson Leland taught me is that *I had to change myself and my perfectionism.* Together with him, I was forced to face and accept autism. And I felt I had to tell the world what autism is and what autistics can do. Frequently, I heard the same hurtful comments at Leland's exhibitions, "This is a painting from an autistic? How can the painting have such a high price tag?" "He is a third-generation heir of Café Astoria. His family is rich and can afford to cultivate him." When I hear those conversations, I tell myself I can't withdraw into misery; instead, I continue to smile and swallow my indignation at the same time.

Leland helps me see the huge difference among people and their unjust point of views. If we can't learn to understand, tolerate and respect each other's differences, it is going to be a cold and cruel world. I know that on this journey I have much to learn along with Leland.

# Everyone thought I was insane

From the moment I decided to move 17-year-old Leland with me from the U.S. to Taiwan, everyone thought I was crazy. From their point of view, I was separating my family, since Jason and my husband Philip remained in Los Angeles. What was most shocking to them was that I actually planned to pluck an autistic child, born and educated in the U.S., not able to speak Mandarin, and put him in a brand-new environment.

The general consensus is that autistic children need to stay in a familiar environment in order to live a stable life. A tiny change in the daily routines of autistics is so disruptive that they can't function, let alone adapt to a country where a different language is spoken. They asked, "You are not afraid that this can be detrimental to Leland? Have you really thought this through?"

Of course, I knew the consequences! But I heard a loud inner voice that I needed to go back to Taiwan to take care of my parents. Besides, there was a fire at Café Astoria that year. I didn't have the heart to let my parents face the disaster alone. The voice of "Go home!" was louder than everything else. I prayed and believed that God would bless my decision.

Despite everyone's disapproval, I moved Leland to Taiwan. I took care of my frail parents and sick brother, took over Café Astoria and put up a tough fight against a local construction company's urban renewal plan. The urban renewal plan would have made Café Astoria disappear from its current location—along with its legend.

When the circle of parents in Taipei with autistic children found out I had returned to Taiwan, many came to Café Astoria wanting to find out Leland's "success" story and my parenting experience. There was a period of time when Café Astoria turned into a consulting center!

Generally, Taiwanese parents with autistic children keep things quiet and just accept their fate. Parents don't think their kids will have break-throughs. They feel hopeless and resign themselves to the fact that they will spend their entire life providing care. Leland's presence in Taiwan becomes a a symbol of hope to these families.

Taiwanese parents frequently ask, "Why is Leland always smiling, always happy?" Leland surely doesn't smile all the time, he also has moody moments, but he probably smiles more often than other autistic children. Why?

*Rodeo Cowboy I*

Because I do my best to fill his days with activities; I tell him his daily schedule so that he always has activities to do.

There is another frequent question which surprised me. "How can you look so elegant?" Unfortunately, the self-images of parents with autistic children are distressed and ragged, like homeless dogs. My appearance is probably elegant but that is an expectation I set for myself. I don't want Leland to see a sloppy and distressed mother, even if my mind is desolate. The toughest time was when my mother, my father-in-law and my brother were all in hospitals. To take care of them, I went to three different hospitals, kept Café Astoria running and took care of Leland. That time was the darkest and loneliest in my life.

Praying when I get up every day gives me my daily strength. The first thing I do every morning is to read the Bible and let God's words pour into my heart. Thinking back on those dark days when the future was so bleak, the stress I had was unimaginable! But my faith gave me strength and made me believe in myself, that I, along with Leland, could make it through the toughest time. Even now, I still live in God's love and grace every day.

*Wait! Mommy, 2013, 29" x 36", acrylic on canvas.*

# There is no tomorrow

*Leland giving a speech at the 2014 Training the Talent of Artists with Autism art exhibit and V.I.P. auction.*

Leland can write and has good hand-writing. I started teaching him how to write daily diary since he was 5-6 years old. At the beginning, he couldn't write on his own, so we wrote together, word by word.

One day when I was exhausted, I fell asleep as soon as I laid down on the bed. I often dozed off while reading words to him. When I couldn't stay awake, I would ask him to finish tomorrow morning.

To my surprise his reply was, "There is no tomorrow." When I woke up the next morning, Leland had finished his diary on his own. Once this habit was established, he wouldn't go to bed until he wrote in his diary, even if it would take 30-60 minutes for him to finish.

I had always taught him, "Don't' put off things to tomorrow when you can do them today." I am never sure how much Leland understands conversations but occasion-ally he surprises me with his words. That's right, why wait till tomorrow? We have to live like there is no tomorrow, to live our lives to the fullest.

To this day, Leland maintains the diary habit. Every night, he writes down everything that has happened that day. He has accumulated some 30-40 diaries in his room, which may be one of the longest journals in anyone's life.

One time I was chatting with a friend, who was in tears complaining about her husband and marriage problems. All I could do was comfort and support her. Leland was sitting there quietly and suddenly said, "It doesn't matter. It's all in the past."

*Taiwan Embassy, Paris.*

That line is from an animated Disney film, The Lion King, one of Leland's favorite animation movies. He watched it over and over for many years. Sometimes he just watches specific scenes. I didn't know that the dialog had quietly taken root in him and that he had the ability to use those words in proper situations!

Things that we assume he doesn't absorb, he actually listens to and absorbs; things that we think he doesn't understand, he actually understands to some degree.

Throughout his life, Leland will probably need conversation lessons and keep a diary every day. He will progress very slowly in everything he does. Yet, as long as he is motivated, how can I ask him to give up?

The desire of learning is built into everyone's genes. As Leland said, "There is no tomorrow." Maximize every day and put your best foot forward! Don't be discouraged when you encounter setbacks. "It doesn't matter. It's all in the past."

# The power of learning

Moving to Taiwan meant Leland had to start from zero. With no friends or schools willing to take him, I decided to do home-schooling. I hired a tutor, who used The Mandarin Daily News, a local newspaper, as reference, teaching Leland phonetic symbols and Chinese conversation. Surprisingly, he learned the phonetic symbols really well! It's probably because of his Taiwanese heritage, or inheriting linguistic talent from his grandfather. Leland dispelled the doctor's prediction that it was impossible for Leland to learn a second language. But this miracle would not have been possible if it weren't for the long-term endeavor of nonstop teaching and learning for the previous ten years.

Leland started to recite poems from the Tang Dynasty in Mandarin with a heavy American accent.

Before my bed a pool of light,
I wonder if it's frost aground.
Looking up I find the moon bright,
Bowing, in homesickness I'm drowned.

       – In the Quiet of the Night


By the hills the sun loses its glow,
Into the sea the Yellow River flows.
To gain a three-hundred-mile view,
Keep climbing up a floor to view.

       – Up the Stork Tower

Leland even inserted several classical poems from the Tang Dynasty into his paintings. My guess is that he probably relates to phonetic symbols and Chinese characters as drawings.

In Taiwan, he also learned guitar from scratch. The guitar was a going-away gift from Dr. James C. Yu, an elder from our church in Los Angeles. With a grateful heart, we took the instrument on our plane and brought it to Taiwan. But where could I find a teacher?

*Blue Jazz, 2014, 50" x 38", acrylic on canvas.*

*Leland plays guitar at an event.*

When I had been living in the U.S., through my church connection, I had opened my home for dinner every Thursday night to young students from Taiwan who were studying in the U.S. One day in Taipei, a young man came to Café Astoria and asked for me, saying his name was Jerry. Jerry had been one of those students who came to dinner. I asked him what he was doing since he returned to Taipei and he replied that he was studying music at a Taipei college. "I teach guitar lessons," he added. God even sent a guitar teacher for Leland!

Leland grew up in a musical environment, but I had no idea if he was capable of learning guitar. However, he became enamored with it once he started playing. Whenever we scheduled a lesson time, I had to find an afternoon when Jerry didn't have other obligations. Otherwise, we would run into a situation where the student wouldn't let the teacher leave and the teacher had to rush out to his next class. If Leland couldn't learn a song well, he wouldn't quit and wouldn't let Jerry go until he managed to learn it and Jerry would say Leland's playing was good. *There is no tomorrow* is Leland's famous saying. There is no tomorrow, so he has to learn it today.

Fast forward from learning guitar to now, when Leland can play and sing more than one hundred English, Mandarin and Taiwanese songs. On one Mother's Day, he wrote a song for me expressing his love and gratitude with a simple melody and lyric. Some say autistics don't have a soul.

When hearing Leland's pure and innocent voice, I see an angelic soul. Unfortunately, his physical form is a mismatch to his soul.

Many churches invite Leland to perform. One time he sang Amazing Grace at a church event where everyone was impressed and moved. I watched Leland with tears in my eyes and thought his life is so enriched and perfect. Why do people still see him as broken and incomplete?

The second lesson Leland taught me is *the power of learning*. With proper guidance and opportunities to learn, he is like a sponge, absorbing everything you teach him. Life is a journey of endless learnings. Regardless of one's background and environment, we move forward as long as we make our best effort in learning. Even if we stumble, we would have no regrets. I never had regret about moving back to Taiwan.

One day, I asked Leland, "Do you like Taiwan?"

"I like it," he said. He liked Café Astoria, the crowds on the streets, the trains and the high-speed rail lines. The only aspect he doesn't like is the endless number of "square" or boxy buildings in Taiwan, where architecture lacks warmth and an aesthetic quality. Leland's instinct doesn't lie.

After moving back to Taiwan, parents with autistic children frequently asked me, "My child has been learning for so long. Why haven't we seen any progress?" Also, "If he has been learning for so long and makes no progress, should we let him continue? Is it a waste of time and money?"

I always reply with this question: "How long has your child been learning?"

Some people say six months, while others say a year. But is that enough?

*Photos by film director Zheng-Cheng Lin during an interview for the 2009 documentary, Twinkle Twinkle Little Star.*

*Blue Nose, 2008, 16" x 20", acrylic on canvas.*

There are parents whose children have severe autism; they can never learn or they repeat the same things as if they are a broken record; therefore, the parents give up hope in teaching them any-thing. These parents are advised that it's best for their children to stay home for the remainder of their lives. Just like that, many kids with severe autism are de-prived from learning.

On the contrary, my point of view is these children deserve to have more chances to learn due to severe autism. They must keep practicing and repeating what they have learned. Apart from his talent in painting, everything else that Leland does, such as brushing his teeth, washing his face, going to the toilet, talking, reading, horseback riding, swimming, playing ball and keeping a diary, are incredibly hard for Leland. He learns everything in the slowest way. Everything needs to be taught repetitively for a long period of time, which doesn't mean one or two years but 5-10 years - or even longer. If you persevere for 5-10 years, you may see a tiny bit of progress. Give the children five years or ten years and they will show you some improvements.

From my perspective, if the learning window is less than 5-10 years, it's not long enough. We are not pursuing medals or recognitions. This endeavor is extremely lonely and we can't see the end. Despite the hard-ship, we must put in the efforts. Otherwise, if we don't try our best, life is meaningless.

As an example, use Leland's experience to learn how to speak. Despite having English and Chinese conversation classes every day, he still can't carry a conversation in which the content is a bit more complicated. He only understands the direct meaning of words. He can politely say "Hello" and can hug and greet people with no problem.

He can also reply to easy questions:

"How are you?" "I'm fine."

"What are you doing today?" "Leland paints."

"What do you paint?" "Leland paints moose."

"Why moose?" "Leland likes moose."

Whenever someone compliments his paintings, he smiles and replies, "Thank you."

For now, that's the extent of his conversation ability. But he keeps making progress.

*Dragon, 2014, 16" x 16", acrylic on wood.*

# It's important to have good health

The third thing Leland taught me: *One must be in good health to live a life and deal with endless trials and tribulations.*

Ever since he was a child, Leland doesn't sleep much. He wakes up at daybreak every day and never dozes off during the daytime – just like a fully-charged battery. One time he went biking with friends; everyone stopped on the next block and turned around. He kept riding to the next town! We had to chase him in our car.

In 2009, when we were filming the Twinkle Twinkle Little Stars documentary with Director Zheng-Cheng Lin in Paris, we were at Notre Dame de Paris. The director wanted to shoot a scene at the top of the cathedral, although there were more than three hundred steps! The director said, "Leland, you can lead the way!" This decision was a mistake, since it took Leland practically no time to walk to the top while the crew and I were huffing and puffing. We kept hearing him say "Where are you? Where have you gone?" I kept pushing myself to reach him, I was so worried about him being alone at the top for too long.

At the time that we visited the Great Wall of China, Leland's energy was a nightmare for me! We went to Beijing for an Asia Pacific Conference on Giftedness. My friend drove us to the Great Wall for an afternoon visit. The weather was bad. When we got off the gondola lift that took us up to the wall, we walked a while and came upon a forked road: one direction was the way back to the gondola while the other direction led to the end of the path. But it would take seven days to reach the end! Leland was so impressed by the Great Wall's magnificence that he became obsessed with it and insisted on taking the longer way. I refused and told him our friend would have to wait for us for a long time.

"That's fine. Just let him wait," he grumbled.

"It will take too long." I said, but it didn't work. Leland has no concept of time, so I can't explain that how long is "very long." If I say one hour, he can't connect one hour with "very long."

"We have to finish this today," he said. "There is no tomorrow."

He headed straight to the longer route and I had to run after him. There was no one around. The uneven and bumpy road made running harder and

I was out of breath. As the sky got darker, it felt gloomy and scary. All I could do was to curse Emperor Qin Shi Huang for building the Great Wall!

Leland was way ahead of me. He turned around and asked, "Mommy, why you are gasping for air?"

"Mommy can't catch her breath," I said.

"It's ok," he said and kept walking! When a gust of cold wind blew in, I was shaking and couldn't even stand straight.

It's in Leland's nature to keep walking to the end if no one stops him. I had to distract his attention to make him turn around. I told him we were going to see a performance in the evening. On that day, we passed by eighteen guard towers in total, which took us three hours. He had to walk to the top of every tower. At the top, he gesticulated excitedly with his hands, his way to make new memories. The next day, my legs were incredibly stiff. I had even worn out my shoes!

*Flower, 2013, 24" x 36", acrylic on canvas.*

Perhaps this is a lesson I have learned on my own: *the necessity to be strong mentally and physically in order to accompany Leland on this life journey.*

# Live in the moment

Among all the lessons Leland has taught me, the most precious is *having a pure heart*, the kind of innocence that comes from deep in one's heart.

According to Dr. Oliver Sacks, the development of the human nervous system is most incredible. From childhood, we have been influenced or forced by customs, traditions and society to receive various teachings and trainings, as well as obeying laws and conforming to the political environment. Competitiveness in school and in the workplace forces the brain to develop towards an unnatural developmental pattern of reflexive restriction.

Therefore, people learn to embellish, conspire, lie, play games, connive, play double-cross, keep hidden agenda and deceive each other. People lose their innocence and this world becomes ill-minded. Autistic children happen to dodge all the badness, they maintain their innocence.

Leland has the talent in drawing but he has no ego, no clue about fame and wealth. His favorite thing in the world is ice cream. He likes chocolate, vanilla and cranberry flavors. The only thing he wants to buy with money is ice cream. The interesting part is, he only eats one scoop each time. If one scoop is $1.60 and two scoops are $2.90, most people would buy two scoops, but he still insists in having just one scoop. He has no concept of money, let alone knowing what a bargain is.

Leland can describe everything wonderful through ice cream. "The ice cream-like summer breeze," he says like a poet. But the truth is that he probably smells ice cream in the summer breeze. When he had an exhibition at the city hall in Paris, Taiwan's ambassador to France visited and praised Leland's paintings. I heard the following conversation:

"Your paintings make us really happy. How about we invite you to Paris again next year?" the ambassador asked Leland.

"No." Leland said. Leland's reply embarrassed me.

I asked him "Why not?" since I believed he had his reason.

"I'm in Paris now. There is no next year!" he said.

*A church in Rouen, France.*

Usually, in response to invitations to return, whether out of politeness or because we actually meant it, we would reply, "Yes, I'd love to." This agreeable response is a standard social interaction. But Leland doesn't understand these. His thinking is, "I am right here in Paris, why do you ask me if I want to come here next year? What does it mean?" Right now, this moment is the only and most important thing for Leland. He is not worried about tomorrow. He doesn't think about the future.

But life is not that simple. We think about going to Paris when we are in Taiwan. When we are finally in Paris, we think about Taiwan; there are always matters that need attention at home. There are always problems that can't be solved. We always think about what are we going to do next, where are we going to eat next, what will be like tomorrow. We are never satisfied and we are always planning. We sink into nonstop thinking, endless troubles and constant desires.

On that day, Leland taught me the most important lesson: *Live in the moment.* Just enjoy the sunset by the Eiffel Tower. We are in Paris now, aren't we? We have to live to the fullest and seize every moment.

Occasionally his directness can put people on the spot. One day, I took Leland to visit his grandfather at the ICU. He looked at his grandfather on the bed and asked, "Is grandfather going to heaven?"

Fortunately, his grandfather still kept his sense of humor. He said to Leland, "Grandfather will go to heaven but not today."

Unexpectedly, Leland kept asking, "Not today. But when?" We were thrown out of the ICU by Grandmother in less than three minutes.

A funny incident happened in France. We were invited to a high-end steak restaurant where we had to dress up. A couple of minutes after the steaks were served, the waiter came and asked, "Sir, how do you like the steak?" Leland replied in a very polite way, "I flew ten thousand miles for this shit." I almost spit the water out of my mouth! But I had to be composed and stayed elegant. Leland learned that line from the movie Rush Hour 2. He loves that movie as much as The Lion King. He has watched them over a hundred times and can recite all the dialogue.

Most importantly, his response was perfect, although with unintended humor. The steaks they served were tiny and dry. I was muttering but didn't dare to complain. Surprisingly, Leland replied in such a brilliant way! Thanks to Leland we were all served new steaks.

After the Twinkle Twinkle Little Stars documentary was released, Leland became more famous. People started to recognize him on the subway and asked for his autograph. Unfortunately, our schedule was often very tight, sometimes we didn't have time for everyone, so people were disappointed. Did Leland become arrogant from fame? Of course not! How can he be arrogant when he doesn't understand arrogance?

In 2012, NBA star Jeremy Lin was invited to Xinzhuang Sports Arena. I took Leland to pay "homage" to the NBA player who generated a global craze known as "Linsanity." Everyone wanted to shake hands with Jeremy but no one could get close to him. When Jeremy went backstage, Leland had to use the toilet. It was a pure coincidence that they met face-to-face in the men's room. I watched them from a distance.

Leland said to Jeremy, as if he saw an old friend, "Hi, Jeremy." Jeremy didn't know what was going on. "Who's that guy?" Jeremy probably thought Leland was cool. But to Leland, Jeremy Lin has been a friend. His pureness and straightforwardness make him enjoy every moment of his life. It's simply natural to say "Hello" when you come across an old friend. People tend to judge others by their own point of view all the time. What we see is actually the reflection of ourselves. We lose our innocence by exploiting the imperfections of others.

*Banana Guitar Elephant*

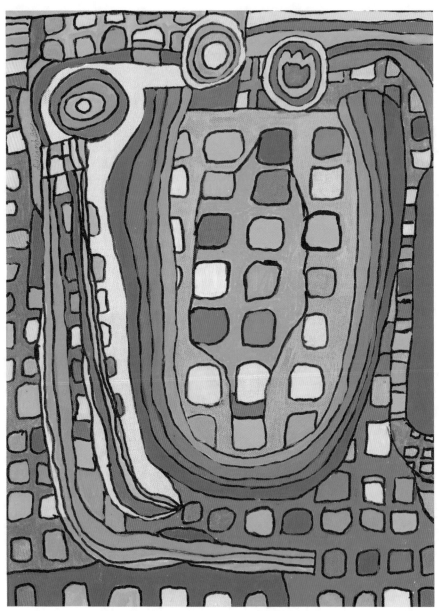

*Taipei MRT, 2013, 29" x 36", acrylic on canvas.*

# When they grow up

Who suffers more, a patient with autism or the patient's family?

Once I read a case from a book about an autistic child who had learned to wait for the green light before crossing the street, but that lesson was limited to the street in front of his house. When the child was brought to the street in front of his grandparent's house, he would dash across without paying attention to the traffic light. He needed to be taught again, from the beginning.

I was surprised to learn our environment is full of hidden dangers for autistic children; they seem to live in a wilderness where they might be devoured by beasts anytime. Throughout the school years, Leland attended five funerals of his classmates. Some of them died in car accidents, some of them died from medicine misuse or even human negligence. They didn't get the chance to grow up.

According to some statistics in the U.S., many autistic children die between ages 15-17 due to active secretion of hormones during those teenage years, and difficulty in controlling emotions that can lead to fatal incidents. For a normal person, the hustle and bustle of crowds and traffic are part of the norm. But for autistic children, there are many dangers looming that they can't recognize.

U.S. statistics show that among death by unnatural causes, many cases are autistic patients, half of their deaths are caused by their parents. The truth is cruel – but we have to face it.

One day, my worst nightmare came true: Leland disappeared.

He had been going to classes at National Taiwan University of Arts in Banqiao. While waiting for the bus to go home, his companion received a phone call and moved slightly away to talk on the phone. Leland turned around and didn't see her. He couldn't ask for help, didn't know to look around or stay put. His instinct told him, "Walk! Walk home on my own."

He walked for five hours – more than twelve miles – from afternoon to evening.

As soon I heard the bad news from his companion, I called the police. Friends and relatives helped with the search. I heard that a radio station broadcast the missing-person news. Those five hours felt like five centuries for me. I prayed and prayed. All I wanted was for Leland to be safe. When he walked home, the moment he was in front of me, the tears that I had held for five hours burst like a flood. I asked him how did he find his way.

"God brought me home," he said.

There will be one day when I will no longer be able to protect him. But before that day comes, I have to train him to be independent as much as possible. I will find him a nanny who loves him and is reliable, I will make sure he is not alone later in life. No one can replace a mother. But a mother isn't an immortal.

I have to take him to see and to experience everything while I still have the strength and still can move about. I like to see him being happy and laughing. I would give everything in the world to see him smile with the purest joy. I have a simple belief: when everyone says you can't do this or that way is no good, I do it regardless, I keep moving forward. I believe that God will look after those with pure faith.

I don't know how many more years Leland can paint, I don't know if he will still be famous next year, I don't know when invitations to hold art exhibits will stop. The only thing I know is whether he can paint or not, whether he is an artist or not, whether there is someone appreciating his art or not. I will always be his mother and my love for him is unconditional. The families of autistics are all the same around the world. They have their deep pain and sadness, they don't know what tomorrow will bring, but we all do our best. When we are desperate and want to give up, it really means we are seeking help, looking for support to continue.

*New York Landscape, 2013, 18" x 24", acrylic on canvas.*

# A mother's promise

The spring before Leland's 25th birthday was lively and full of blessings. That season was a memorable spring for me. In April 2014, I took Leland to New York City to participate in a significant event called Training the Talent of Individuals with Autism, with keynote speaker Temple Grandin, Ph.D. It was a charity art exhibition organized by Pace University and Strokes of Genius. The organizers invited five artists from around the world to raise money for autistic children.

Leland represented Taiwan. First we flew to Los Angeles, where Jason joined us to attend the event together. We were all excited to see Temple Gradin again. More than ten years ago, it was Temple who reminded me not to focus on the child's disability but to focus on his ability. Years flew by, Leland had grown up. I'm no longer the mother who takes away his paintbrushes. I have become the mother who accompanies him to attend art exhibitions worldwide.

I gave Leland's latest art catalog to Temple. She was so happy! She told me Leland was exactly the same as she saw him last time, except he was much bigger, but he still had his bright eyes and brilliant smile.

During the event, I invited Temple to Taiwan for the 2016's World Autism Awareness Day on April 2nd. I was looking forward for her to come to Taiwan to share her life experience to help more people to discover the talents of autistic children. I gave pineapple cakes from Café Astoria to Temple. She promised me that as long as she is healthy, she would visit Taiwan in two years to see the colorful and beautiful country that Leland portrayed in his paintings. I told Temple that if she comes to Taiwan, I would certainly take her to Café Astoria to taste the freshest pineapple cakes and enjoy a cup of the legendary Astoria coffee, whose recipe has been passed down for over seven decades.

In looking at the 66-year-old Temple and the 25-year-old Leland, I was moved to see them making efforts to help autistic children. Leland was blessed to work together with the well-respected Temple. And I am so blessed to have met Temple back when I was anxious and confused. She gave me the strength to regain courage.

At the venue, I saw Temple's mother accompanying her and keeping an eye on her from a distance. Temple had already beat autism and become a well-known professor with her mother's support, but her mother still stays by her side.

What kind of power gives an 87-year-old mother to be her child's pillar, never leaving her child in seventy years?

I think I know the answer.

Tears were in my eyes. I could imagine seeing Leland in the future, more mature, walking towards me from a distance with the same innocent look and confident smile.

> *Dear Leland,*
>
> *This is the promise between you and me. I will stay with you just like Temple's mother. My steps will become slower and slower but I will accompany you to wherever you want to go.*

*Flower Expo, 2012, 36" x 29", acrylic on canvas.*

*Leland's birthday pizza party at Café Astoria.*

# Every year on May 29th

Leland would mark important dates on his calendar, including Mothers' Day, Fathers' Day, Christmas, Halloween, Thanksgiving, New Year's Eve, Chinese New Year and his birthday.

When I moved Leland to Taiwan, he was seventeen years old. On May 29, 2013, he celebrated his 24th birthday. The average life span of autistic children is 15-17 years; Leland had beat the statistic and scored one more year. I'm so grateful.

On this day, Leland insisted on inviting many friends to come over and make pizza. These parties have become his birthday ritual. We host a pizza party on the third floor of Café Astoria every year on his birthday.

Due to his sensitive auditory nerves, sounds drifting in the air that we barely notice can be a real torment for Leland. I relate to the world full of noises that Leland is in as if I was in an enclosed space and sound was blasting at a high decibel.

So in recent years, Leland had been using earbuds to cancel out noises at home, at Café Astoria, on the street or in an airplane. At 11 o'clock, he had already put on his earbuds to welcome guests.

Every guest was invited by Leland himself: Bao-Ru Ji, Xue-Er, Pastor Xiu-Xia Pan, Dr. Susan Gao, Professor Boris Kuo; Jerry the guitar teacher; good friends, You-Cheng Xu, Yin-Yin Shi, Sue Babcock; and a bunch of friends around his age from Tainan, a city on Taiwan's southwest coast: Annie, Richard, Pearl, Wei-Ting, Jack, Ariel, May, Van, Ching Heng, and Albee.

The top two guests on the invitation list, his grandfather and grandmother, couldn't attend that year. We had a scare at home in the morning: Grandfather was sent to the hospital because of low blood sugar. When he was carried into the ambulance, he held my hands and said to me in a weak-but-firm tone, "Don't worry about me. Just go celebrate Leland's birthday."

I was torn in half. Half of me was standing at the venue with Leland to welcome guests. He could say everyone's name and hug them. Half of me was so worried about my father in the ICU.

At twelve o'clock, I got the phone call from Grandmother. She said that Grandfather was stable so I didn't have to worry. She also told me it wasn't necessary to go to the hospital and all I had to do was to have fun with Leland at his birthday party.

The birthday party was joyful and lovely. Leland received many well-wishing cards. Everyone rolled pizza dough, added their favorite toppings, scribbled their name under the plate and sent it to the kitchen. One-of-a-kind, customized pizzas were created, one after another.

As far as Leland is concerned, his birthday is the most important day of the year. He starts to work on the guest list one month in advance, on a big piece of paper. He lists names according to the person's importance to him. Grandfather and Grandmother are always on the top of the list. Then, I make phone calls with him. If someone says he or she will be occupied on that day, Leland would grunt to show his discontentment and cross off the name.

"I have tests." "I have a meeting." "I broke up with my girlfriend, so I don't feel like going out." Leland will never understand people's excuses.

One year we flew home from Europe a few days before his birthday. I was so exhausted that I just wanted to rest. I didn't have the energy to plan the pizza party. On his birthday, there were friends calling to wish him Happy Birthday. I guess Leland thought that people would be at Café Astoria to make pizza as usual.

But no one was there. He only saw Grandmother taking out a little birthday cake. "Where's everyone?" "Where's everyone?" he kept asking. He was anxious and almost broke down, obviously distraught with the fact that his birthday party had been bypassed. What should I do? I had no choice but to call a few friends. They were such troupers that they took leave from work and came immediately.

In a nutshell, you just can't tell Leland that you are busy on May 29, so let's celebrate in advance or have fun in a different way. We must get together and make pizza on that day.

At the party, I watched Leland from a distance. He is a one-of-a-kind child, calm and focused on the pizza dough in front of him. He used the rolling pin to make the dough round and thin as if he was painting. I imagined the mental state that he was in at that moment, he must have felt like a fish swimming in the sea.

LeLand Lee

LOVE is

LIFE

李 柏 羲

Our pastor led everyone in prayer. I thanked God for letting Leland have another birthday, for taking care of my father in the ICU, for being my pillar when I lost my strength and couldn't move on. He raised me up and led me onward to today. Then the highlight of the party was everyone singing Happy Birthday and waiting for the birthday boy to cut the cake.

A 24-year-old man is supposed to be an independent grown-up. When Leland's brother, Jason, was 24 years old, he could already drive his brother and me in southern France. Leland is different. When it comes to painting, he is a genius. But otherwise he has to learn nonstop and repeatedly. Things that others learn in one month take him one, two or even three years. Learning for Leland is like getting an intravenous injection, the fluid goes in slowly. He can never stop learning. We make progress little by little.

Like everyone else, Leland still has many undeveloped potentials. But living independently, dealing with a world constantly changing, facing complicated interpersonal relations, or learning rules of engagement that change all the time will be an impossible dream.

As for dreams, I once had one in which Leland had gone back to being a kid. He walked to me while talking to me. I was frightened and broke down crying. Then I woke up and saw him sleeping on the other side of the room in the darkness. He had already grown up. I looked at his big body; he was breathing normally. I felt relieved that the scary scene was nothing but a dream. I didn't have to start over.

I am aware that autistic children face different bottlenecks at different ages. I can only pray to God and ask for wisdom and courage in order to face the daily challenges. But I don't have the courage to look back on what I have been through. Nor do I dare to imagine the future. I only want to seize every moment, every day.

God didn't give Leland the ability to communicate normally; however, He gave Leland a pure heart and blessed him with the extraordinary gift of artistic talent, through which he communicates. Through his paintings, he also introduced Taiwan to the world: its scenery, friendliness and liveliness.

Like a shadow, I will always accompany Leland. I will be by his side and watch him document every moment, every thought and every feeling he has through his paintbrush. I will spend every day with him. . . until there is no tomorrow for me.

*Leland and Karen, Laguna Beach, California*

Karen Chien was born in Taiwan and grew up in her father's famous Café Astoria. Karen has two children, Jason and Leland. She lived in Los Angeles for 29 years and returned to Taipei to run the family business. She tirelessly advocates for autism, raising awareness for parents and the public to focus on children's abilities instead of disabilities. Karen coordinates Leland's art exhibits and other appearances around the world. She especially enjoys going to Moscow with Leland and her mother, where Karen is always looking for new Russian recipes to offer at the café.

Leland Lee has had wide recognition, such as receiving the 10 Outstanding Young Persons Award from the Junior Chamber International (JCI) Taiwan. He has participated in international councils, conferences and symposiums, and been featured in a documentary film.

"There is no tomorrow" is Leland's favorite line. He captures moments in life through his paintbrushes. Leland's art gallery is available at his website: www.lelandlee.com.

Leland x Astoria, a smart phone application using Augmented Reality (AR) technology, is available for free at the Apple Store and Google Play. When using the app's Scan Art feature, a set of special AR artworks appear with animation.

Karen and Leland currently reside in Taipei, where he works at the legendary Café Astoria, a bakery and restaurant serving Russian coffees, Russian-based pastries, western-style cakes, wines and cuisine. The recipes for Russian soft candy and mazurka are based on the original recipes used for the Russian royal court. Those treats are Astoria's signature pastries, loved by adults and children alike: www.facebook.com/astoria1949.